"Hating you was pure and simple,"

she whispered. "It was black and white, no room for pain. But I can't hate you anymore. I don't want us to be enemies." Unshed tears burned the back of her throat.

He pulled his hand away from hers and laid it on her shoulder. Through the sweater she could feel the warmth of his skin. "You want me to be your *friend?*"

"You make it sound so awful!"

He laughed as if he were teetering on insanity. "I can't wish you good fortune and watch as you marry another."

"Why not?" Liquid flames shot through her veins, making her dizzy.

"Because my thoughts aren't the least bit friendly toward you." His gaze pinned her. "Every time I look at you, I want to strip you down naked and make love to you."

* * *

The Lightkeeper's Woman
Harlequin Historical #693—February 2004

MARY BURTON

The Lightkeeper's Woman

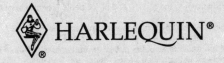

HARLEQUIN®

TORONTO • NEW YORK • LONDON
AMSTERDAM • PARIS • SYDNEY • HAMBURG
STOCKHOLM • ATHENS • TOKYO • MILAN • MADRID
PRAGUE • WARSAW • BUDAPEST • AUCKLAND

ISBN 0-373-29293-7

THE LIGHTKEEPER'S WOMAN

Copyright © 2004 by Mary T. Burton

For Cathy Maxwell and Pamela Gagne,
wonderful critique partners and friends.

Prologue

1882

There was never enough time.

Alanna Patterson stood before the small open portal of the captain's cabin. The night wind was warm and the dark sky aglow with an endless blanket of stars. The gentle waters of James River lapped against the side of the schooner *Intrepid*.

She closed her eyes and drew in a deep breath. Mossy scents of the docks mingled with the aroma of tobacco bundles and freshly milled lumber. The ship had been loaded this afternoon and was ready for departure tomorrow.

If only this night could last forever.

Strong arms banded around Alanna and wrapped her in warmth. Her hand came up to his powerful arms. "Caleb."

He nuzzled his cheek next to hers. Thick stubble teased her soft skin. "Come back to bed."

She tipped her head back against his bare chest. "It's getting late. I must leave soon so that I can be home before anyone realizes I am gone."

Caleb inhaled a deep breath. "I don't want it to end."

Heat spread through her body as she remembered their lovemaking. "Nor I."

"I love our nights together but I hate it when you leave."

"Soon we will be wed and I won't have to sneak back home at dawn."

His arms tightened around her. "Stay with me. Come with me on this next voyage."

The idea tempted but reason overcame it quickly. "I can't leave Richmond now. And you will be back in six weeks. It's not such a long time."

"Six weeks is a lifetime." He laid his large hands on her shoulders and turned her to face him. She stared up into his warm blue eyes so filled with love and tenderness. "Marry me."

She flattened her hands against his bare muscular chest. His heart beat wildly under her fingertips.

"We are getting married after you return," she said.

He captured a strand of her silken blond hair between his fingers. "The ceremony is not for three more months. I want to marry you now."

She smiled. "It's the middle of the night."

"There's a church not four blocks from here. I'll wake the minister."

The idea made her giddy. She traced the cleft in his chin with her fingertip. "We can't wake the minister, Caleb. It wouldn't be right."

His gaze darkened. "Why not? I'll make a large donation to the church to make it worth his while."

She sensed an edge of desperation in him that she'd never felt before. "My father wants to give us a grand wedding as a peace gesture. It's his way of giving us his blessing. And my mother would have wanted the best for me if she were alive. I don't want to disappoint him."

"We'll marry again before everyone if that's what you want, but tonight I want to marry you."

She took his hands in hers. His calluses rubbed against her smooth palms. "Why the sudden change?"

He shoved out a sigh. "Call it a bad feeling."

She traced his firm jaw with her fingertip. Seamen put a good deal of stock in omens and gut feelings. Even Caleb, as logical as he could be, wasn't immune to superstition. "There's nothing to worry about. Father has given his blessing. There's nothing to keep us apart anymore."

"I want the world to know you are mine. I love you more than anything. If I were to lose you, I'd go mad."

She squeezed his hand. He wielded great strength in his body, yet he allowed her to see the vulnerability in his heart. "I don't need a minister's vows to seal my love for you. I will be waiting for you when you sail back into the harbor six weeks from now. I am yours. I will love and honor you, Caleb Pitt. Forever and always."

"Forever and always." He dropped his gaze to their hands clasped together. He kissed her fingers. "Say it again."

"I will love you forever and always, Caleb. I am yours to the end of time."

"And I love you, Alanna. For richer or for poorer, in sickness and in health. Until death us do part."

Tears filled her eyes as she stared up into the face of the man she loved. "Nothing will ever tear us apart."

Chapter One

Two years later

The coachman set the brake and shouted, "Easton, North Carolina."

Alanna Patterson pushed back the stained coach curtain and stared at the meager collection of gray-black buildings made of sunbaked wood. The town's main thoroughfare was little more than a path etched into the sandy mud by wagon wheels. The few fishermen and women standing alongside the street looked as tired and broken as the buildings. As if they too had weathered too many winter storms and too many hot, humid summers.

Why in God's name would Caleb have chosen such a place to call home now?

Alanna had last seen Caleb on the deck of the *Intrepid,* his ship, as it headed out to sea. She'd been so proud of him. His blue sea captain's jacket had been tailored perfectly to fit his tall frame and broad shoulders. His pants molded his muscular legs braced against the sway of the ship. He'd been smiling, waving toward her as he'd tried to shout her a few final words. The wind had drowned out his baritone voice, but she'd not worried. She'd gifted him with a vibrant smile and waved. She'd been so confident that their charmed future would be filled with many loving words that a few lost ones wouldn't matter.

What a fool she'd been.

Unsettled, Alanna gathered her velvet skirts as the coachman opened the door. The tall, gaunt man took her elbow as she climbed down. Her soft gray leather boots sank into the mud up to the laces.

"My shoe!" Alanna said. "Couldn't you have at least put down a plank?"

The coachman's gap-tooth grated her nerves. "Everybody knows fancy duds don't last in Easton."

Alanna pulled her foot from the sucking mud. The shoe's pale leather would forever be stained brown. "In your line of work *as a coachman* I would think you'd see many people who aren't from Easton. And that you'd *take the time* to tell them about the streets.''

He shrugged as he took her bag from the coach. ''Strangers don't come to Easton unless they's shipwrecked. Most folks who've been pulled from the sea is so happy to be alive they don't care so much about their shoes.''

Most probably hadn't paid as much for their shoes as she had hers.

Alanna reached for her bag. ''Thank you for your help,'' she said tersely. ''But I can manage from here.''

He tugged the bag and brought her a step closer to him. This close, Alanna could see dirt coating his pockmarked face. She could smell the hint of cheap gin and stale fish on his worn clothes. ''I notice there ain't no one here to meet you.''

She remembered how hastily she'd packed her satchel. ''My arrival is a bit of a surprise.''

The coachman's lips twisted into a grin. ''That so? I'd be happy to help in any way I can. Name's Roy Smoots.''

Alanna didn't miss the implied proposition woven between Smoots's words. Another time, another place she'd have reminded him of his place.

But, as he'd said, she was alone. "No, thank you."

She yanked her bag free, stumbling back in the slippery mud a step before she caught herself, her derby-style hat slipping over her right ear.

He laughed. "Sure I can't help?"

Righting her hat, she said, "Just tell me where I can find Rosie's Tavern."

The coachman didn't look offended, but more amused. "A half a block down the street. I'd be happy to show you."

"Don't trouble yourself, Mr. Smoots." Alanna stepped through the thick mud, cursing her ruined shoes.

Mr. Smoots fell in step beside her. "No trouble at all."

Ignoring him as best she could, she stepped onto the boardwalk and stamped the mud from her shoes before she started down the sun-baked planks. Her bag thumped into her heavy skirts with each step.

The tavern was a two-story building marked by a faded wooden sign with black scripted letters that spelled Rosie's below a faded red rose. The sign and building looked just as weary as the rest of town.

Alanna reached for the rusted handle. "Mr. Smoots, when does the next coach leave Easton?"

Mr. Smoots's grin widened. "I leave at first light."

"Book a seat for me. I'm leaving this town as quickly as I can."

"Sure thing, miss." He cackled. "So what you doing tonight?"

Alanna ignored the question as she shoved open the tavern door. She paused, letting her eyes adjust to the dim light. Sea spray and grime clouded the inn's small windows and blocked out the noonday sunshine. Around the room, two dozen fishermen stared at her over their tankards. Most had full beards and skin as weathered as the boardwalk.

The seamen's whispers buzzed around Alanna's head and their gazes darkened with a dangerous hunger. Her palms began to sweat in her kid gloves and for the first time she realized just how truly alone she was.

These were the kind of men Caleb had sailed with. Though he'd respected his men as sailors, he'd always been careful to keep them away from Alanna. And now she understood why.

Mr. Smoots circled his fingertip on her shoulder. "Sure you don't want ol' Roy's help?"

Alanna flinched and pulled away. "No, thank you."

He leaned so close that she could feel his hot breath on her ear when he spoke. "Don't say I didn't warn you."

Mr. Smoots brushed past her, knocking her shoulder with his as he moved toward a table in a darkened corner where three other sailors sat. He said something to the men and they all laughed as they stared at Alanna.

Alanna could feel her courage slipping. When she'd received Caleb's terse message days ago the urge to right old wrongs had burned hot. Time and fear had cooled the fire in her.

The barkeep, a burly man with a belly that hung over his belt, looked up from the glass of gin he was pouring. Surprise flickered as the barman set down the bottle and moved from behind the bar toward her.

Lantern light flickered on the white strands of the barman's red beard and a gold loop hung from his left ear, winking in the lantern light. His crooked nose looked as if it had been broken more than once. He grinned as he wiped his hands on his soiled apron. "Name's Sloan. Can I help you?"

Alanna's mouth felt as dry as cotton as Sloan's

gaze slid up and down her body. Her fingers clamped tighter around the handle of her valise. "I'm looking for Captain Pitt," she said in a soft voice.

All traces of humor vanished from Sloan's face. "Who'd you say?"

Just speaking Caleb's name left her edgy and restless. "Caleb Pitt," she said in a louder voice. "Do you know where I can find him?"

The tavern room went deadly quiet and the men who'd been staring at her looked away.

Sloan's eyes narrowed. The innkeeper studied her and she had the sense that she was being tried and judged. She wondered briefly if Caleb had told him about her. The old Caleb was a man who'd always kept his own counsel, but the new Caleb was a stranger to her.

"He ain't in town," Mr. Sloan said.

The tension that had been knotting her muscles frizzled into anger. "I thought he lived here in town. He listed Easton as his address."

"He lives here sometimes, but he ain't here now."

"Then where can I find him?"

Mr. Sloan nodded toward the front door. "It's best you leave."

Alanna couldn't go back to Richmond, not

when she was so close to settling matters once and for all. "I've traveled too far to turn back."

The innkeeper started back toward the bar. "Cut your losses. Leave."

Alanna lifted her chin up. "I'm sure someone will tell me where I can find the captain if I wait long enough. I am willing to pay," she said a little louder.

Alanna looked around the smoky room. Slowly, the men started to talk among themselves, and she had the distinct impression she was their topic of conversation. A minnow among sharks, she thought vaguely as she tapped her foot and counted the seconds until she could leave.

She moved into the room, aware that Mr. Sloan watched her as she walked toward a chair at an unoccupied corner table. Sloan hurried across the room. "What do you think you're doing?"

"Sitting down." She nodded toward a wobbly chair. "Aren't you going to pull back my chair for me?"

At first Sloan stared at her. Then, sighing, he yanked the chair out from under the table. "Rest your bones a few minutes, and then I want you gone."

Alanna gifted him with her best smile and sat

down, her back to the wall. She took a moment to adjust the rich folds of her velvet skirts.

Bracing a hand on the back of her chair, he leaned forward and said in a low voice. "I know who you are and I can tell you that the captain don't want anything to do with you. Do yourself a favor and leave the past buried."

Heat burned her cheeks and stomach. How many times had she prayed the past would just go away? But each time happiness was within her grasp, bitterness and anger spawned by a thousand unanswered questions swept it away.

Unshed tears burned her throat. "I've no choice in the matter. I must find Captain Pitt."

Mr. Sloan shook his head as he straightened. "Too bad."

Alanna almost laughed at the irony. For two years she'd avoided the idea of facing Caleb. Now when he was so close, she met one roadblock after another, almost as if the fates didn't want her to see him.

She folded her hands in her lap. "I'm not leaving until I see him."

The innkeeper shook his head. "It don't work that way here, missy. You tell me what you want, then I'll decide if I talk."

Sighing, she realized she'd have to give Sloan

a little information. "My father passed on recently. He left the captain a package, and I'm here to deliver it to him."

"What kind of package?"

Alanna pulled a small teak box from her cape pocket and set it on the table. It measured six inches by six and was fastened tightly with a polished brass lock. It was the same box her attorney had mailed to Caleb, the same box he'd returned. "This kind."

A bit of the wariness faded from Sloan's sharp gaze as he stared at the box. "Give your parcel to me. I'll run it out to the island the next time I take the captain's supplies."

Alanna remembered Caleb's terse response to her letter. *I want nothing from you or your father. We are finished.* The fire that had driven her hundreds of miles from home burned anew. "I intend to deliver it to him myself."

The creases in his leathery face deepened as his eyes narrowed. "Ain't this desire of yours to see him a little late?"

So, Caleb had told Sloan who she was. Defensive, Alanna raised her chin. "There are things you don't know."

Mr. Sloan shook his head as he appraised her. "You're trouble."

"If you think your unwillingness to help will chase me away, you are very wrong. One way or the other, Mr. Sloan, I'm going to see the captain."

"Suit yourself, but you'll get no help from me or anyone else in this village." He turned and walked away.

Alanna rose, her napkin clutched in her hand. "Mr. Sloan!"

"You won't find anyone to take you."

"I've no intention of causing trouble for the captain."

He waved away her words.

Frustrated, she glanced toward the bar where five seamen openly stared at her. In a voice loud enough for all to hear, she said, "I need someone to take me to the barrier. And I'm willing to pay."

Realizing she'd addressed them, the sailors dropped their gazes into their tankards.

"None of them will do it," Sloan said from behind the bar.

"I just want to give him this box, then I will leave him in peace."

"Leave the captain alone," a sailor shouted.

"Aye, he's a fine man who don't need the likes of you messing up his life," another sailor said.

She stared at the roomful of grim faces. "I mean him no harm."

"Go away," several sailors shouted.

Shocked by their anger she turned to Sloan. "I just want to give him this box."

Sloan shook his head. "Since the captain's been manning the lighthouse, he's saved a lot of lives. Everyone in this town can claim a friend or relative who's been rescued by the captain. That's all anyone in Easton cares about. I can tell you now no one will take you to the captain."

She opened her mouth, ready to argue, when she caught sight of a seaman moving away from the bar toward her.

The man was a weather-beaten old salt who wore loose-fitting pants, a stained shirt and pea jacket that smelled of fish. He'd tied his long gray hair at the nape of his neck with a piece of frayed rope and sported a bristly beard that reached halfway down his chest. "You really looking to go to the outer banks?"

Alanna hesitated. Rougher than Mr. Smoots, the man looked like a pirate and likely had the morals of one. She wouldn't have considered his offer if she weren't in such a hurry to return to Richmond. "Yes."

Sloan's scowl darkened. "Get back to the hole

you crawled out of, Crowley. The lady don't need your help.''

Alanna bristled. ''Don't listen to Mr. Sloan. I do need to book passage to Barrier Island.''

The seaman set his half-full tankard of ale on her table and sat down. ''Let's talk then.''

Sloan cursed. ''Don't be a fool, lady. This ain' the kind of man you want to deal with.''

Alanna took her seat. ''Thank you, Mr. Sloan, but I can take care of myself. You may go now.''

Sloan stared at her. ''You is as hardheaded as Caleb says. Fine, go with Crowley. You two deserve each other.''

Alanna's heart pinched. Caleb had said she was hardheaded? She wanted to ask Mr. Sloan what Caleb had said about her, but pride wouldn't allow it. Working the tightness from her throat, she shifted her gaze to Mr. Crowley. ''Can you take me to the outer banks, Mr....''

The old man stared at her as he sipped his ale. ''Ain't no Mister. Just Crowley.''

''Alanna Patterson.'' She was grateful her voice sounded steady.

''I'll take you across the sound, if you're paying.''

Alanna tightened her hand around her reticule next to her plate. ''I'm offering two bits.''

Foam from his ale clung to his mustache and beard. "Make it five dollars."

Her mouth dropped open. "Five dollars! I don't have that kind of money!"

Crowley eyed her rich cape trimmed with a thick brocade border. "Fine. Find someone else." He started to rise.

Alanna knew he was likely her last chance to see Caleb again. Clearly no one else in town was offering help and soon she'd be married and there'd be no going back. She dug out a rumpled bill from her purse. "I'll pay you one dollar."

Crowley paused. "I can't hear you."

Fearful others would hear she carried cash, she lowered her voice. "All right, two dollars. But it's all I have left."

He sat back down. "Done."

Alanna pushed the dollar across the sticky table toward him. "I'll give you the second dollar when we return."

She thought he might balk at the condition as he took the bill and sniffed it. Satisfied it wasn't counterfeit, he tucked it in his pants pocket. "Deal. My boat's called the *Sea Witch*. She's moored on the docks alongside the other boats. Meet me there in the morning."

"I can't wait that long. I must return to Virginia tomorrow.'' Tension crept up Alanna's spine, goading her to explain. ''I have appointments I must keep.''

In truth, Henry had forbidden her to talk about Caleb. If she weren't back by Friday when Henry returned from his trip to New York, he would realize where she'd gone and follow. He'd be furious.

Crowley shrugged. ''Meet me at the docks in thirty minutes.''

''I'll be there.'' After Crowley strode out of the tavern, Alanna wrapped the box in oilcloth and shoved it in a side pocket of her cape. She closed the flap to the pocket and fastened the single button closed.

Soon, she'd be standing face-to-face with Caleb. Her stomach churning, she consoled herself with the idea that this time tomorrow it would all be over.

''You ain't planning on sailing with Crowley, is you?'' Sloan's sharp voice made her head snap up.

Alanna bristled at his tone. ''As I said before, it's none of your business.''

A hint of worry deepened the lines around Sloan's eyes. ''Even a woman like you don't deserve the likes of Crowley.''

Pride had her digging in her heels. Since her father's suicide a year ago, she'd grown accustomed to taking care of herself. She'd faced down creditors, seen precious heirlooms sold and watched her world crumble. "Thank you for your advice. But I can take care of myself."

"Go home where you belong."

Unsettled, a part of her wanted to explain this journey was the hardest she'd ever undertaken. She'd lost weight, not slept well in weeks. She simply wanted to be free of the past and memories of Caleb once and for all.

But she didn't say any of those things. Sloan was right. She didn't belong here. And the sooner she completed her task, the better. "I've come too far to turn back now."

Chapter Two

Alanna walked the two blocks to the piers jutting into Currituck Sound's restless waters. On the sandy shore, she watched shallow-bottom boats tied to the docks, bobbing like corks in the black-green water. Their sails were lashed to the masts, a sign that the fishermen expected bad weather.

Never in a hundred years would she have pictured herself standing here waiting for a boat to take her to see Caleb.

Her love for Caleb had been like a wildfire, brilliantly hot, overpowering and destructive. What they'd shared, no matter how delicious, was not meant to last.

Yet, here she stood.

Henry had been asking her for months to marry him, yet she continued to put him off. Finally, she'd accepted. She had a wonderful man in

Henry. He'd remained at her side after her father's suicide and had begun courting her when none of her old friends would receive her.

Henry checked on her daily, he worried over her and made her feel safe. If she married him, he would see to all the details. She'd never have to worry about money again and her life would return to what it once was—petted and secure.

So why hadn't she said yes?

She turned to the sound. The bits of sunshine that had peeked through the clouds moments ago had vanished. Erratic winds swooped through the reeds trimming the shoreline, making them sway and bend. An osprey flapped its wings and landed in its nest atop a wind-stunted oak.

The weather was closing in. She and Crowley would have to move fast if they were to make the journey before the storm hit.

It seemed even the heavens were warning her to keep away from Caleb.

"Best we get moving," Crowley said as he brushed past her.

Alanna watched the old man limp down the peer. He seemed confident enough about the weather and making the crossing. After all, if it were too dangerous he wouldn't make the journey, right?

Determined, she picked up her valise and

stepped onto the pier. Bracing her feet she accustomed herself to the movement. Water lapped against the moorings as she tiptoed down the dock, careful not to get her heels caught in the wide openings between the boards.

The vibration of her footsteps had Mr. Crowley raising his head from the rope knot he was untwisting. He snorted. "Hurry up. We ain't exactly got all day."

She stared at his vessel that was as weatherbeaten as her pirate captain. Her sail was patched in a half-dozen places and water sloshed over the bottom. "Is there supposed to be water in your boat?"

Crowley unfastened the rope from the dock. "The *Sea Witch* is an ocean-worthy gal and she's never failed me."

Doubt had her lifting her gaze to the sound. A handful of whitecaps dotted the waters. "The water looks rough."

He shrugged. "I've seen worse."

She nibbled her bottom lip. "Would it be better if we waited an hour or two?"

"Women. Couldn't make up their minds if their lives depended on it. I thought you was in a rush? Look, if you don't want to go that's fine. But I'm not giving your dollar back."

Her gaze lifted to Caleb's lighthouse on the

north end of the outer banks. It seemed much, much closer. The guilt and anger she'd carefully kept locked away for two years pounded at her heart. She was so close. "I have to go."

"Then the water's calm enough." His eyes narrowed. "You bring the money?"

"I'll give it to you when we return."

"Fair enough." He twisted his thin lips into a half smile. "Don't worry, the *Sea Witch* will serve us well. Now if we are going to shove off we best do it now."

Now or never.

Alanna handed her valise to Crowley who tossed it toward the bow of the boat. It landed in a puddle of water on its side. "Would you please right my bag? I don't want my things getting wet."

He didn't spare the bag a glance. "With these waves and wind, we'll both be soaked by the time we reach the banks."

Alanna hesitated. Was anything to go right on this journey?

"Move your fanny!" Crowley said.

Sighing, Alanna lifted her hem. Careful not to snag her skirt, she climbed down the small ladder into the boat's damp bottom. The dinghy wobbled from side to side as she clung to the ladder. It was one thing to look at the boat from the dock, quite another to stand in the leaky vessel. She doubted she'd have let go of the pier if Crowley hadn't pulled her roughly onto a wooden plank seat.

"Women and the sea is a bad mix," he muttered.

The rocking boat unsettled her stomach. She wished she'd thought to pack crackers or a piece of bread. It still wasn't too late, she thought in a panic as she stared at the dock. She could leave this wretched place behind.

The box buttoned tight in her cape pocket brushed her leg, a reminder of why she was here. "It's been a couple of years since I've been on the water."

Crowley studied Alanna's white-knuckle grip on the side of the boat. "You ain't gonna panic or worse start crying is you?"

She lifted her chin. "Of course not."

He studied her an extra beat as if he half expected her to cry. "God save us all."

The old seaman took his seat across from her, his back facing aft. His knees brushed hers and she could smell the strong scent of whiskey. Gripping the oars, he pushed away from the dock.

Despite his age, Mr. Crowley was a strong rower and within minutes they were a hundred feet from shore. He paused long enough to raise the sails. The boat started moving at a fast clip.

Frigid northeastern winds smelling of salt and sea teased the curls peeking out from her hat and flapped the folds of her cape and skirt. The water grew choppier, and she lost sight of the dock.

Now that they were out of land's reach, the lighthouse seemed miles away. A wave broke over the bow of the boat, spraying her face with seawater. Sputtering, she wiped her face clean. If the boat were to overturn, no one would be there to save her. She would simply vanish into the sea.

"I hear twenty-three men died when the *Intrepid* went down in a storm. The survivors say the ship's boiler blew without warning."

"Yes, it's true."

He snorted. "A good captain goes down with his men and his ship."

How many times had she heard others in Richmond utter the same thing? Ironically, Caleb's reputation would have fared better at the inquest if he had died with his men. But Caleb had been blown free of the *Intrepid* when the boiler exploded. In the maritime world he'd done the unpardonable—he'd survived when his men had died.

And then her father had supplied the reports that stated Caleb had refused maintenance on the *Intrepid*'s boiler so he could leave port three days earlier. His fatal error had killed twenty-three men.

She'd been so ill those weeks after the accident. Weakened and exhausted, she'd broken their engagement in a fit of grief and fear. Her father and friends had told her over and over that she'd made the right decision. As her health improved and she grew stronger she'd started to question the events surrounding the accident. Caleb had always seemed so careful when it came to his ship.

Her father had discounted her doubts and then without warning he had shot and killed himself in his study. The devastating loss had left her in a state of shock for months. When she finally let go of her grief, she came face-to-face with the reality—her father's business wasn't simply in trouble—it was gone. She was penniless.

"What are you to him?" Crowley said.

"An old friend," she lied, hoping he'd leave her to her thoughts.

Crowley grunted as his narrowed gaze skimmed slowly over her. "You and he were *friends?* Lovers maybe, but not friends."

The old man was right. Alanna and Caleb had loved each other; they had laughed together; and yes, they had been lovers, but they'd never been friends. So caught up were they in their attraction to each other, they rarely discussed anything other than the most superficial.

Perhaps if they'd been better friends, he'd have told her more about his business. In the months after the disaster, she replayed their conversations over and over. She'd searched for any clue that might have helped her understand why he'd set sail without repairing the boiler. Dear Lord, if money had been his problem, she would have sold her jewelry for him. But as hard as she thought back, all she could remember were comments he'd made about her hair, her wit or her pretty clothes.

Crowley asked other questions about Caleb, but Alanna offered vague answers, unwilling to talk any more than was necessary. Soon the two lapsed into silence.

As she watched another wave crash over the bow of the boat, her mind drifted to the Caleb she'd known and loved. She'd been drawn to him the instant she'd first seen him firing orders at the men in the shipyard. For the first time in her life, she disobeyed her father and strode out onto the Patterson's Shipping docks, determined to meet him.

They'd been drawn to each other like lightning to water. From the outset, the passion that had burned between them seemed eternal.

The roar of thunder brought Alanna back to the present. The memories receded but as always they never quite went away.

She'd tried to rebuild her life and suddenly wondered if Caleb had done the same. It tore at her to think of him with another woman. He could well be a father by now. "Mr. Crowley, has the captain married?"

"No."

A small part of Alanna's heart eased. "Because of the *Intrepid*?"

Crowley's hands tightened around the oars as he dug the paddles deeper into the water. "That's part of it."

"Have you seen him lately?"

For a moment he didn't speak, his full attention on the water. "Been a few months."

"Does he look well?" She hated her curiosity.

He stared at her as if she'd asked a foolish question. "As well as can be expected."

"Does he spend most of his time at the lighthouse?"

"He's a regular hermit."

Lightning sliced through the clouds. The old man shifted his full attention to the sky that had grown suddenly very dark. Fat rain droplets mingled with the wind and the boat started to pitch.

Alanna's lips tasted of sea salt. She glanced

down at her cold feet and realized the water had risen up to her shoelaces. "The boat is sinking!"

Caleb stared out the lightkeeper's cottage window, relieved to see the thunderclouds rolling over the horizon. An unexpected restlessness had been building in his bones for days. Normally, he'd have attributed the sensation to the onslaught of bad weather. Reading the weather was an extra sense for him, as much a part of him as sight and touch.

But since Sloan had delivered Alanna's package last month, his well-ordered world had tipped out of balance.

Caleb's heart had raced as he'd held the package wrapped in brown paper. With his fingertip, he traced *A. Patterson* emblazoned in the upper left corner.

"Who is she?" Sloan had asked.

Caleb's lips twisted into a grim smile. "How do you know it's a woman?"

"Your jaw's so tense it's liable to snap." Sloan grinned. "And a man don't fondle another man's package."

Caleb grunted. "We've supplies to unload."

Sloan didn't move. "So who is she?"

Caleb wondered if fire still spit from Alanna's jade-green eyes when she was angry; if her hair still spilled down her back like spun gold. "Nobody."

Sloan rubbed his bearded chin with the back of his hand. "Right."

Caleb held out the box. "Take it."

Sloan looked at the package as if it were hot coals. "What do you want me to do with it?"

"Throw it in the sea for all I care."

"No note?"

Caleb had been cheated out of his last confrontation with Alanna and his mind swam with a thousand unsaid words. He pulled a pencil from his coat pocket and on the box's brown paper wrapping scrawled: *I want nothing from you or your father. We are finished.*

Sloan accepted the box from Caleb and studied the message. "You loved her, eh?"

Caleb's head started to throb. "I was cursed by her."

Since Alanna's parcel had arrived, the island which had been his sanctuary had become brutally small. He'd paced the shores like a caged animal. He worked as hard as three men, but no matter how much he'd sweat, he couldn't exorcise Alanna from his mind.

Twice, he'd nearly abandoned his post and rowed to the mainland.

But he'd stayed on guard.

Lightning flashed.

Caleb shifted his focus to the gray horizon. Aye, he'd take a storm over Alanna any day.

He grabbed his coat, shrugged it on and headed toward the lighthouse. With the storm brewing, he'd have to light the beacon.

Crossing the small sandy beach, he entered the base of the lighthouse and climbed the spiral staircase up to the top. Ever ready, he kept the giant Fresnel lenses polished, the lamps filled with oil and the wicks trimmed. And now as the blue sky had vanished behind the thickening clouds, all that was left was to light the lanterns.

Caleb rechecked the lenses that magnified the light for dozens of miles, and then climbed down a small interior staircase that led outside to the crow's nest, the wrought-iron balcony that ringed the top of the lighthouse.

Wind howled around him as he reached in his pocket and pulled out his spyglass. Opening the telescope, he scanned the ocean horizon. There were no ships and if luck held none would venture this close to the shoals, sandbars that stretched the length of the outer banks, until the storm passed.

The danger of the storm was far from over but as he stared at the endless waters he felt a measure of calm. Unlike his days in Richmond, he was in his element here. He understood storms and he understood the seas. Here actions, not words, solved problems and saved lives.

He moved around to the sound side. He didn't expect to see a boat. His assistant, Charlie Meeker, had gone into Easton yesterday on a four-day pass. Charlie had sense enough not to brave the waters today as did Sloan, who had only come to the island three days ago to restock supplies.

Only a fool dared these waters today.

And the world was full of fools, he thought grimly as he raised the spyglass on the remote chance that someone would attempt a crossing.

Caleb peered through the telescope lens. For an instant, a slash of white appeared in his scope but it disappeared behind a wave as quickly as it had appeared. A man with lesser experience would have attributed the sighting to a whitecap.

But he waited, holding his glass steady. He understood just how deceitful the sea could be, so he waited.

When waves rolled down, the splash of white peeked above the wave again. There was no mistaking what it was this time—it was a ship's sail. "Who the hell would be out there today?"

He looked closer. Instantly, he recognized the *Sea Witch*. Crowley, of course. Like a vulture the man came out from under his rock each time a ship went aground. The old bastard had also done his share of gunrunning and smuggling during the war. But there were no shipwrecks to scavenge. And Crowley never made a crossing unless the money was good.

"What is that old bastard up to?" he muttered.

The waves pitched higher, and the boat bobbed in the water like a buoy. Caleb knew that soon the rains would grow heavy, swamp the boat and capsize it.

"I should leave you to the waters, you old bastard." Caleb touched the small scar on his temple, remembering his last encounter with Crowley. The bastard had tried to kill him.

Crowley shifted his position to lower his sail, now straining against the wind. That's when Caleb saw the trim figure of a woman.

An oath exploded from Caleb as he squinted harder. Though wind and fog blurred her face, he saw the crop of golden hair, like a beacon in the storm.

His gut clenched.

There was only one woman he knew who was foolish enough to travel in this kind of weather with Crowley.

Alanna Patterson.

The daughter of the man who'd ruined him.

The woman who'd betrayed him.

Chapter Three

Howling winds filled the sails and tipped the boat dangerously out of balance as waves crashed over the bow. Alanna watched the icy water slosh back and forth in the bottom of the *Sea Witch* and clutched the boat's rim as it dipped closer to the briny water. "Mr. Crowley, are we sinking?" she shouted over the wind.

He muttered an oath and hauled himself to his feet using the mast as support. Bracing his feet, he glared at the taut white sail as he unleashed the rope and let out the canvas. The boat righted herself instantly, but the thick sails snapped and fluttered wildly.

"Mr. Crowley," Alanna repeated. "Are we sinking?"

"Just a bit of water. Don't get all hysterical on me."

She lifted a drenched boot. "The water is up to my ankles."

He shot her a sideways glance. "Then stop your complaining and start bailing."

"With what?" Alanna searched around the boat but found nothing to use.

"You got two hands," he shouted.

Fear crept up Alanna's spine as she cupped her hands and started scooping handfuls of water out of the boat. She glanced up at the blackening sky. "Is the weather getting worse?" She heard the squeak of panic in her voice, but was beyond caring if Crowley thought she was a coward. She was afraid.

"What do you think?" he bit back. "Of course it's getting worse." Crowley wrestled the thick, flapping sail as if it were a wild bronco down to the wet boat bottom.

Alanna discovered that despite her frantic bailing efforts the water was getting deeper. "You said this boat was seaworthy!"

"She is. Mostly." The oars scraped against the oarlocks as Crowley buried them into the choppy water. His muscles bunched and strained as he fought to assert his control over nature.

"*Mostly?*" Panic burned through her veins. She started bailing again. *Oh God, Oh God.* What had she gotten herself into? "Tell me we aren't going to sink."

"We're not going to sink."

"Do you mean that?"

"No."

Alanna closed her eyes. If only she'd stopped to think this trip through. If only she hadn't been so impulsive, she'd be safe at the inn or, better, in Richmond.

She remembered how quickly she'd left Richmond. She'd left a note of course, but she'd lied to Henry's aunt and told her she'd gone to Washington. "No one knows we're out here."

A wave crashed into the side of Crowley's face and he spit out a mouthful of water. "If we sink, it won't matter who knows what. We'll die anyway."

She glanced toward the lighthouse beacon. Clouds shrouded the island's shoreline, but its light flashed bright. "How far is the shore?"

Worry had deepened the lines on the old man's face. "Too far."

Her clothes were soaked, and the cold was seeping into her bones. "Do you think *he* knows we're out here?"

"If he does, he'll not raise a finger to save my hide."

Her teeth started to chatter. "Why not? That's his job, isn't it?"

"We had a run-in a few months back."

Could this get any worse? "What kind of run-in?"

"I tried to kill him."

Alanna didn't ask for details. They didn't matter now.

If she'd worked all day to select the most dangerous of circumstances, she'd not have done as well as she'd done in choosing to cross the channel now with Crowley.

The inky waters filled the boat. The rim sank closer to the water's edge. A crack of lightning streaked across the even blacker sky.

Alanna's soaked cape hung on her shoulders like lead and she couldn't feel her toes. "I don't want to die, Mr. Crowley."

Droplets of rain dripped from his wrinkled face. His eyes no longer glowed with anger or frustration, but fear. "Who does?"

Frigid water drenched Caleb's pants as he shoved the dory into the churning sound. The rowboat bucked in the wind, pushing back toward shallow water as if it, too, understood that only fools went out in weather like this.

"Goddamn you, boat, move!" Frustration ignited his rage. Caleb hated losing. Even more, he hated losing to the sea.

Cursing, he blew out a breath and focused on the set of notches he'd carved into the boat's bow. The seventy-six portside marks denoted rescues. The twenty-three on the starboard side commemorated each man he'd lost when the *Intrepid* had gone down not far from these very shores.

He drove the boat deeper into the water and jumped aboard. Taking the oars in his callused hands, he rowed toward the spot where he'd last seen Crowley's tattered white sails.

"Damn her. Damn her. Damn her," he chanted as he rowed. "The Devil take them both." Crowley was a thief and a liar, and Alanna wasn't much better. Impulsive as ever, Alanna did what was best for Alanna without a thought to whom she endangered.

Anger sidetracked him and, for a moment, he couldn't find the rhythm of rowing. He drew in several deep breaths. This rescue was like any other, he reminded himself. It was about beating the sea at its own game. It didn't matter whom he saved, only that he won the game.

Drawing on sheer will, he set his gaze starboard and moved his arms in a steady tempo. One, two. One, two. As the wind howled in his ears, his muscles took over.

Caleb concentrated on the roar of his heart and the burn in his well-conditioned biceps as they pumped the oars. Currituck Sound was determined to make him earn every inch of forward progress today, but he'd never walked away from a fight. Hot sweat trickled from his stocking cap, warming skin chilled by the wind.

A woman's scream pierced the rain and mist. He turned and caught sight of Crowley's boat just as a wave crashed over it. The swell caught Crowley broadside and knocked him over the side.

Alanna clutched the side of the *Sea Witch* but by some miracle she wasn't swept into the water.

Caleb dug the oars deeper into the water, coaxing more speed from his boat.

No one had been lost since he'd been on watch at the Barrier Island Lighthouse. No one! And he'd be damned if Alanna Patterson would be the first.

"Mr. Crowley!" Alanna's wet skirts twisted around her legs as she scooted toward his side of the boat and wedged her feet under the seat in front of her. She pushed her rain-soaked cloak off her shoulders and held out an oar. "Grab on!"

Alanna watched the old seaman flail in the water. His hat gone, he smacked his palms against the water, trying to keep his body afloat. But each time he reached out for the boat, the water pushed him back. He dipped under the surface once, then came back up gasping for air.

He reached for the paddle. His bony fingertips brushed the smooth wood as a wave smashed into him and sent him under the surface. Tense seconds ticked as Alanna searched the water.

''Don't die on me!''

The old man was drowning, and it was her fault they'd come out here. She should have waited until tomorrow. Why hadn't she just waited?

Mr. Crowley's head popped to the surface a good five feet from the boat. He gasped for air and spit up a lungful of water. Desperation tightened his face as he reached again for the oar she held out. His fingers dug into the smooth wood like fishhooks and he pulled himself closer to the boat.

Alanna struggled to keep the paddle steady. She strained against his weight and fought not to tumble into the water herself. Her limbs burned from exertion. The cold had sunk to the marrow of her bones. ''I can't hold on much longer.''

He spit out a mouthful of water. ''Pull, woman, pull,'' he yelled. ''I ain't ready to die yet.''

Her breath was labored, and she fought against the weariness slipping into her bones.

Crowley pulled himself closer to the boat and

then swung one hand over the rim. He drew in a deep breath and struggled to pull himself in the boat. "Grab my belt, woman!"

Alanna dropped the oar and reached for Crowley's thick belt. Angry wind blew rain sideways, but she tightened her numb fingers around the leather and pulled him up. He lifted one foot up on the side of the boat and yanked himself out of the water.

She felt a tremor of elation. He was going to make it back into the boat. He would get them to shore. Everything was going to be fine.

A swell of water from the north blindsided Alanna. The unexpected shove to her overextended body threw her off balance. She tried to right herself but she tumbled over the edge of the boat into the water.

Her open mouth and eyes filled with seawater and for dark, tense seconds, she flailed around, not sure what was up and what was down. Her skirts weighed her down and her lungs ached for air. Forced to tap into energy she'd never known she possessed, she kicked and battled the sea.

Alanna burst through the surface. Her arms smacked against the choppy waters and she struggled to keep her face above water long enough to breathe. Air filled her lungs. She was a strong swimmer, but her clothes made staying afloat in the choppy water next to impossible.

Salt water stung her eyes, blurred her vision. She focused on the *Sea Witch*. It bounced on the water just out of her reach. "Help!"

Crowley glanced in her direction and scanned the waves.

"Help!" she shouted. "Over here."

For the briefest instant his gaze locked on her. And then he turned away.

"I'm here!"

Crowley sank the oars back into the water and started to row away from her toward the mainland.

Barely able to stay above water, she raised her arm to signal him. "Help! Mr. Crowley, don't leave me."

The old seaman rowed away from her as if he hadn't heard her plea.

Had the wind drowned out her voice? "Help!" *Please save me.*

Her legs and arms neared exhaustion. She started to sink. She gulped in a mouthful of water.

The idea that she might die stoked her anger and made her fight harder. But her fury was no match for the numbing cold. She slipped under the water.

Her lungs begged for air, but she knew the next

breath would fill her lungs with water, not air. How long could she hold on? Thirty seconds? Forty?

There was so much she'd done wrong in her life. She should have found it in her heart to forgive Caleb. She should have tried to understand him better. She should have listened more closely to her father during the days before his suicide.

Let me live. I swear I'll make amends. I'll never miss church again. I'll give more time to the poor.

Please, I don't want to die.

A viselike grip wrapped around the collar of her dress.

Death had come to claim her.

She clawed at the hand and kicked her legs wildly. She would not go into the underworld without a fight.

But her body was beyond exhaustion and Death was too strong. It pulled her through the water.

Then suddenly, she broke through the surface of the water. Air! She sucked in oxygen as rain pelted her face. The hard edge of a boat scraped against her belly before she unceremoniously landed in the bottom of a boat.

Alanna collapsed on her side, coughing. Chilled to the bone, she lay still for a moment as she filled and refilled her body with oxygen. Slowly, her mind cleared enough for her to realize she was safe.

"Mr. Crowley?" she said, her eyes still closed.

"Crowley's gone." Anger tinged a raspy voice.

"Where?"

He draped a worn blanket over her shivering body. "Back toward the mainland."

Her teeth chattering, she clutched the rough blanket with trembling hands. So cold. "He left me."

"Yes."

She huddled under the blanket. "Am I dead?"

"No, you're very much alive."

She nearly wept with gratitude. "Thank you."

Black-booted feet braced on either side of her. "Don't thank me yet. We're far from safe."

She opened her eyes. Rain dropped on her face, making it difficult to focus.

Her rescuer's face was turned toward the lighthouse's steady beacon, but she could see that he was dressed in a heavy black coat and wore a stocking cap. His shoulders were broad, his legs powerfully built. Large callused hands gripped the oars.

Tears tightened her chest. What little strength remained, the cold now sapped. Struggling to think, she closed her eyes and slipped into unconsciousness.

* * *

Caleb glanced down at Alanna. Curled on the bottom of his boat, she was breathing, but she looked painfully small and her blond curls were matted against her pale skin.

She'd need warm, dry clothes soon or the cold would suck the life from her. But for now, all he could do for her was get her to shore.

Caleb set his sights on the lighthouse shore. His body was well conditioned to the hard work but soon the winds would be too much for him.

The dory bumped against the sandy shore thirty minutes later. He jumped from the boat and yanked it onto land. Rain pelted his face as he tied the boat line to the moorings of a small dock.

He quickly stowed the oars in the boat bottom and lifted Alanna into his arms. Even with the weight of her damp clothes and cape, he could tell she'd lost weight. Alanna had always been vibrant and alive, never frail.

The years had taken a toll on them both.

The thought offered Caleb no satisfaction as he hoisted her against his chest and started toward the small white-framed cottage just a hundred yards from the base of the lighthouse. A black shutter had come loose from its lock and banged in the wind against the side of the house. A rooster-shaped weather vane atop the roof spun wildly in circles.

He glanced up toward the lighthouse to make sure the light still burned bright. Satisfied when he saw its steady flash, he strode up the five steps to the porch and pushed through the front door.

Water dripped from his clothes and Alanna's skirts as he strode down the darkened hallway toward a back room he reserved for the rescued. He laid her on a bed outfitted with fresh sheets.

Caleb pulled off his wet gloves and lit a lamp and then the preset fire in the hearth. He waited until flames flickered, sparked and spit out the first bit of warmth.

He drew back, shrugged off his coat and hung it on the back of a wooden chair before turning his attention to Alanna.

He raised the lantern. Her damp blond ringlets blanketed her face and her gloved fingers were curled into small fists as if she still fought for her life.

He touched her cheek, needing to reassure himself that she was real. Her skin felt cold, but her breathing sounded stronger.

The wet clothes were seeping the warmth from her body and if he didn't undress her soon, what the storm hadn't accomplished, hypothermia would.

He set down the lamp on a small bedside table and flexed his fingers. His outrage remained as raw as the day of the inquest—the day she'd refused to see him.

Annoyed, he reminded himself that he'd stripped many a near-drowned sailor. And buttons and bows aside, the job remained the same.

The sooner he set about the task, the sooner it would be over.

Lifting her foot, he yanked at the laces of her boots, then tugged each off and tossed them on the floor. "Why couldn't you stay away?"

She moaned softly at the sound of his voice but remained unconscious.

Caleb unfastened the clasp at the base of her throat and pulled off her cape, made five times heavier by the water. He was amazed she'd stayed afloat as long as she had wearing the contraption.

Most men or women couldn't swim, but Alanna's father had had a healthy respect for the sea and had insisted his daughter learn as soon as she could walk.

And she'd always been a fighter.

There'd been a time when he'd known her body intimately. Touching her had been as natural as breathing. Now he felt like an interloper.

Irritated, Caleb stripped off her clothes as quickly as he could manage. He then grabbed a blanket from the edge of the bed and laid it over her. He tucked the folds around the edge of her slim body and moved her to the other, drier, side of the bed.

An involuntary shiver escaped her lips as if she were finally wrestling the chill from her bone. She looked so small, so helpless.

Caleb stood back and dug a hand through his wet hair. His fingers brushed the rough skin of the scar on the right side of his face. "You shouldn't have come."

As he turned to leave, she rolled on her side and curled her knees up to her chest. "Caleb."

Chapter Four

The instant Alanna stepped out onto Patterson Shipping's docks Caleb Pitt had noticed her. He'd also not been happy to see her. Still, Alanna kept walking, drawn like a moth to a flame.

His ink-black pants and cable-knit turtleneck sweater had been as dark as his thick, closely cropped hair. His long, muscular legs had eaten up the space between them in seconds.

"Lady, do you have any idea how dangerous these docks are? Most sailors would eat a pretty thing like you up," he shouted over the winds.

Undaunted, Alanna had stood her ground. "I'm looking for my father, Obadiah Patterson." If she thought dropping the company president's name would intimidate him, she was wrong.

His powerful body blocked the sun as he towered over her. His gaze trailed over her small frame, taking in every detail. "Then you should know how unsafe these docks are for women."

His masculine scrutiny left her body tingling. "I stand corrected." Unrepentant, she held out her hand. "Alanna Patterson."

He pulled off a worn leather glove and took her hand. He squeezed her fingers gently, but she could feel the leashed power in his hand. "Caleb Pitt."

She lifted an eyebrow. "Father's told me a lot about you."

"That so?"

She smiled, confident. "Father says you're rough around the edges, trouble."

Caleb's vivid blue eyes sharpened. He leaned close to her. His own scent mingled with the sandalwood of his soap. "He's right."

She held her ground. "He also tells me a sea witch blessed you with the gift for reading the seas."

Laughter sparked in his eyes. "I'm afraid you've got it wrong. 'Twas not a sea witch that gave me the talent, but the Devil."

She feigned shock. "The Devil?"

"Aye. The talent to read the seas and predict storms in exchange for my soul."

Alanna laughed at his outrageously dark humor. "I've never met a man who sold his soul.

Tell me, would you like to attend a dinner party Father's having on Friday? I'd be very interested to know how one goes about bargaining with the Dark Prince,'' she'd teased.

''I'd be delighted.'' His extra emphasis on the last word made her more aware that with this man she was out of her depth. He possessed an earthy masculinity that, despite her best efforts, left her breathless and blushing.

Alanna's mind drifted in and out of consciousness and sleep. One moment she was on fire, pushing off her blankets, in the next, she froze, unable to get warm no matter how deeply she burrowed under the rough blankets.

But at all times, she was aware of Caleb's rough hands touching her damp forehead, brushing the curls from her head or applying a moist cloth. His deep voice was soft and soothing at times and at other times there were hints of anger. If she'd had the strength, she would have reminded him she was the one that should be angry.

When Alanna finally could open her eyes, she forgot the recriminations. All she wanted was to see Caleb, to know that he wasn't a dream. But through her fever, he remained a dark silhouette, his face shrouded by darkness. The only detail that struck her was that his hair was no longer cropped short. His thick hair, as black as ink, hung past his broad shoulders.

So many things could have been said and all she could think to say was, "You've changed your hair."

He must have thought she'd still been asleep because the sound of her voice seemed to shock him. He drew back slightly. "It's easier."

She moistened her dry lips with the tip of her tongue and closed her eyes. She was simply too tired to connect words into sentences. "That's nice."

She heard the clink of porcelain against glass and the rush of water. The bed's mattress sagged when he sat beside her.

"Drink this." His steady hand lifted her head. He tipped a cup to her dry lips.

She touched his wrist, her hand unsteady. The bitter-tasting drink washed over her dry tongue. It trickled down the sides of her mouth and her neck. "It's awful."

"It's Yaupon tea. It'll soothe your fever."

"If it doesn't kill me first."

"If I wanted you dead, I'd have let the ocean take you."

"Of course."

He pressed the cup to her lips. "Sip slowly," he cautioned. "There's plenty."

"Great." Alanna drank until the cup was empty, then relaxed back against the pillow.

She was vaguely aware when he dipped a cloth into a basin. She heard the water trickle as he wrung the excess water from it.

He pressed the cool rag against her hot cheeks and forehead. The cold felt good. When her skin warmed the rag, he dunked it again in the water. As he ran the cloth over her naked flesh, she realized that she wasn't wearing anything. There was no shame, just gratitude that he was there. Methodically, he repeated the actions until her body had cooled. She slept.

Alanna wasn't sure what time it was when she awoke again, but the room was dark except for the firelight glowing in the hearth.

She was aware of two things. Caleb was still in the room and her thick hair felt greasy and her teeth gritty. "I must look dreadful."

His laugh was bitter, sharp. Her eyes started to focus on him. "If you're worried about your appearance, you'll survive."

Panic exploded inside her at the thought of being alone. "Caleb, don't leave me."

She sensed his gaze on her. "You need to rest."

"Promise me you won't leave just yet. I don't

want to be alone.'' She sounded weak and afraid and hated it, but there was no hiding it.

A long silence stretched between them. ''All right, I'll stay.''

Sighing, she relaxed into her pillow. Feeling more at ease than she had in months, she gave herself to sleep. ''Thank you.''

When Alanna awoke again, awareness of him cloaked the room. She wasn't sure if she'd been sleeping for hours or days. She was only aware that the rain still pelted the windowpanes. A breeze drifted through the open doorway leading to a long dark hallway.

Her head pounded, however, her skin no longer burned and her brain didn't feel fuzzy. She was more like herself.

On the bedside table was the box that had brought her here. Its lacquer coating glistened in the pale light.

Alanna tried to sit up, but regretted the move instantly. Her chest, back and arm muscles ached, the pain a reminder of her struggles in the sound. With some effort, she rolled on her side to ease the discomfort in her back. Her body was stiff, as if she'd aged a hundred years in the last few days.

Caleb. Where was he?

He'd saved her life and cared for her. If not for Caleb, she'd have died.

Few men would have gone into the storm to save her. Crowley had left her behind. Henry wouldn't have had the strength to save her.

When she'd started this journey she'd been filled with righteous anger. In her mind, Caleb had owed her an explanation. He'd owed her an apology. Now, nothing was as clear-cut as it had been. Suddenly, the speech she'd rehearsed and planned to recite seemed juvenile and self-righteous.

Very aware that Caleb was close, Alanna grew restless. She tried to sit up again. Her movements were slower, more deliberate, yet she still winced as she worked her strained muscles and her head spun with another bout of dizziness. Her stomach churned, forcing her to cup her head in her hands.

Slowly her body adjusted to its new position and the spinning calmed. She pushed a curtain of blond hair out of her eyes and surveyed the oversize, partially buttoned white shirt she wore. The shirt was cut wide to fit Caleb's shoulders and, though clean, his scent still clung to the material. Underneath it, she was naked.

Before when she'd been sick, her state of dress hadn't mattered. Now she was very aware of it.

Heat rose in her cheeks as she smoothed her

hand over the cotton sleeves that hung a good six inches past her hands.

"You're finally up." Caleb's rough voice came from a darkened corner.

Alanna started, searching the shadows for him. "Yes."

His face was shadowed and she couldn't make out his features. His long, lean hands rested on the arms of his chair and his legs stretched out in front of him, crossed at the ankle.

On the floor in front of his chair lay a dog. The dog was part shepherd, part mutt with brown-and-black bristly fur. *Toby.* He was older, more muscular, than Alanna remembered, but the crimped right ear was unmistakable. Caleb had found the dog when it was a half-starved puppy living under the Portsmouth docks three years ago.

All she could think to say was, "You kept Toby."

Toby perked up his ears but didn't leave Caleb's side.

"Why wouldn't I?" Caleb's surprise was clear.

She cleared her throat. "I heard your life got…complicated for a while. I just thought the responsibility of a dog was too much."

"I don't run from responsibility." Challenge edged his words.

She might have argued the point with him if

she could have summoned the fire and spit. "I'm glad you kept him. He's a good dog."

Caleb rubbed the dog between its floppy brown ears. His gaze made her skin burn.

Uncomfortable, she fastened the top buttons on the shirt. With as much dignity as she could muster she said, "Thank you for saving me."

"It's what I do," he said coolly.

"Of course." There'd been nothing special about her rescue. He'd been doing his job. The thought that she was no longer unique saddened her. "How long have I been here?"

"Two days."

"Two days! I am expected in Richmond on Friday."

"You always had an active social calendar." Sarcasm etched his words.

Her mind was racing. How could she have slept so long? Lord, she would never be able to explain this to Henry. "I don't suppose you know where my clothes are?"

"Ruined."

Panic shot through her veins. "What do you mean ruined?"

"Water and velvet don't seem to mix, and your underclothes smelled of seaweed."

And her valise remained on Crowley's boat. If Henry were going to be annoyed by her tardiness, he certainly would not appreciate her arriving home half-naked. "Do you have something more dignified than one of your shirts that I could wear?"

He studied her a long moment, staring until she felt her cheeks blush. "I'll scrounge pants and a sweater for you later," he said finally. Clearly, her state of dress was of no import to him.

His lack of concern annoyed her. It also frustrated her the firelight cast a glow on her, but he remained shadowed. She clutched the folds of the shirt tighter. "Could you find something for me now. It isn't proper for me to be half-dressed and alone with you."

A tense silence settled between them. "There was a time when you didn't mind being half-dressed when we were together. Or have you forgotten?"

With aching clarity she remembered everything about their nights together. Too many nights, she'd lain awake remembering the way her skin tingled when he'd kissed the hollow of her neck, how her heart raced when his hand touched her thigh and the completeness she'd felt when he'd been inside her.

He rose to his full six feet two inches. The dog rose and yawned.

Caleb stepped out of the shadows and for the

first time she saw his face. She saw the scar first. Jagged and raised, the scar stretched from the corner of his left eye down over his cheek to his jaw.

Alanna stared at Caleb's scar in stunned horror and then, hating herself for it, flinched. Her father had spoken in passing of Caleb's injuries as if they were little more than scratches.

Her father was wrong.

Whatever had happened to Caleb was violent and agonizing.

She shouldn't have cared that he'd suffered but she did. Tears tightened her throat and several seconds passed before she trusted herself to meet his steely gaze.

Caleb's eyes were the same, blue as a winter sky, but they were sharper, more direct if that were possible. His shoulders looked broader and his hands larger.

The lines around his full mouth and eyes were etched deeper. He'd tied back his black hair, accentuating streaks of gray at the temples. The rugged masculine features she'd once found so appealing had hardened into a chilling, unrecognizable mask.

The anger drained from her face and she felt as if a soft breeze would topple her over. "Did you get the scar in the accident?"

"Yes."

"Caleb, I had no idea."

"Why have you come?" His voice grated like sand against skin.

Color flamed her face. Dear Lord, she should not have come. "I'm honoring my father's will."

"What are you talking about? Your father hated me."

She reached for the box on the nightstand and held it out to him. "This is for you."

He made no move toward her. "You never listened to Obadiah when he was alive. It's hard for me to see you traveling so far to see that his last wishes are observed." He paused. "I can only conclude you came to see me."

The accuracy of his words goaded her temper. "Arrogance was always your downfall."

He nodded his head, acknowledging her statement. "And selfishness yours."

She stiffened.

A low bitter laugh rumbled in his chest. "Let's face it, Alanna. The only person you've ever looked after is yourself."

Her fingers tightened around the box. "How dare you!"

"I'm not in the mood for the wounded dove act, Alanna. I don't want anything from you and especially from your father," he said. "I've already made that clear *in writing.* Or have you forgotten?''

She glared at him, anger burning inside her. How could he be so ungrateful to the man who had brought him into his company? ''Father treated you like a son.''

''When it suited him,'' he said tightly.

''He saw that you met the right people and then, after the *Intrepid,* he tried to protect you.''

Thunder cracked outside. Lightning flashed. For an instant she saw part of his face.

''Is that what he told you?''

''Yes.''

He shook his head. ''Obadiah never let truth get in the way of his goals.''

She set the box back on the nightstand. ''I was right to cut you off two years ago. The man I knew and loved died with the *Intrepid.*''

He moved toward the door, and then paused. ''And may he rest in peace.''

Unexpected tears choked her throat. Fury turned to guilt. ''Henry *was* right. This trip was a fool's errand.''

Caleb's fingers tightened into a fist. ''Henry Strathmore?''

''Yes. And you might as well hear it from me. He's asked me to marry him.''

His shoulders stiffened. His gaze grew very, very cold. "And you accepted."

A shiver traveled down her spine. "I haven't given him an answer."

"But you'll say yes."

She folded her arms over her chest. "I don't know what I'm going to do."

"You'll marry him."

"Don't pretend to know me or my thoughts."

As if she hadn't spoken, he said, "How long was I gone before Henry started sniffing around?"

She watched his jaw tighten, then release, tighten. "Henry has always been a gentleman. He's always been a good friend to me."

Challenge glimmered in his eyes. "What'd ol' Henry say when you told him you were coming to see me?"

The fire seeped from her body. She was silent. As always, Caleb had a knack for spotting weakness.

Caleb laughed, but it held no humor. "I thought so. He doesn't know you're here."

Ducking her head, she touched her fingertips to her temple. It had started to throb. "He doesn't need to know. He'd only worry unduly."

"Right."

As he stared at her, she felt foolish and silly as

if she'd just stepped from the schoolroom. Drawing behind years of training, she summoned her most imperious tone. "I don't appreciate your attitude."

Abruptly, he sighed, as if suddenly all the fight had fled from his body. "I really don't care what you think about me or my attitude. As soon as the storm lets up, we leave for the mainland. And then we can put this miserable reunion behind us."

The dismissal stung. But instead of drawing inward when she was hurting, she did what she always did. She fought.

Ready to stand toe-to-toe with him, she swung her legs over the side of the bed and stood—too quickly. Her head spun. She was going to black out. Her knees buckled. She started to fall.

Strong hands saved her. For a moment, her heart hammered wildly in her chest. She was so aware of his fingers banding around her arms. Of his scent, and of his deep, rapid breathing.

She wanted only to lean into him, to cry, and make the anger between them go away. And for an instant, she gave in to the yearning and leaned her head against his chest.

His heart beat steady and strong. In Caleb's arms, she'd always felt happy and secure.

His body stiffened and for the briefest instant she imagined he leaned closer to her, as if inhaling the scent of her hair. His fingers tightened, and for just a moment, she felt as if the clock had been turned back and they were one again.

He must have felt the same way because he abruptly loosened his hold and drew his face away from her.

Alanna wanted to pull away and stand on her own two feet. Even as her head spun, she reminded herself that she needed distance. Distance from him would allow her mind to clear.

He savagely evoked the memories of the last two years. Those struggles had taught her that the security of Caleb's arms was an illusion. His love had lasted no longer than a puff of smoke or a cloud on a breezy day.

She tried to take a step, but her legs, still too weak to support her weight, wouldn't allow it. Sucking in a breath, she tried once again to pull away. Still, she couldn't manage alone.

As if he understood her struggle, Caleb withdrew a fraction. But he didn't let go of her completely. Like it or not, she needed him right now.

Resigned, she allowed him to guide her down to the bed. She eased back against the mattress, letting it absorb her weight. Lord, but she was tired.

Her eyes closed, she leaned back against the pillow. "My debt to you keeps mounting."

Keeping his head low, Caleb picked up her bare feet and swung them up onto the bed. He covered her with thick blankets, and then retreated toward the door. "You don't owe me anything. We're finished, Alanna." He left without another word.

Chapter Five

Alanna woke in a panic.

Disoriented, she lurched forward in her bed, gasping for air as if she'd been drowning. Dim light trickled in from a small rain-soaked window, casting a murky glow on the simple room more suited for a monk than a lady. No carpet warmed the neatly swept pine floor and other than the bed and nightstand, the only furniture was a single chest and the rocker by the fire.

The room was a refuge but it didn't encourage long stays.

And then she remembered. Caleb. He'd saved her from drowning.

Whatever vague hopes she'd had that all this was some horrible dream vanished. She was trapped on these isolated shores with Caleb.

She remembered Caleb had been with her last

night. When her fever had been so high, she'd been glad to have him close. His touch had offered comfort, but it had also stirred too many buried feelings.

To her relief, he wasn't in the room now. She needed time alone to get her bearings.

Clutching the blanket around her shoulder, she swung her legs over the side of the bed. Instead of landing on a cold floor, her feet came to rest on Toby's tail.

Alanna screamed and jerked back her feet.

The dog's head snapped up, but he didn't growl; instead he studied her, and then yawned.

Her nerves settled, and she felt like a fool for overreacting. Planting her feet on the floor next to him, she scratched Toby between his floppy ears. "Hello, boy."

Toby's tail thumped against the floor in greeting.

"It's been a long time." She looked through the open doorway into the hallway. "Where is he?"

The dog's ears perked.

"Where's Caleb?"

In answer, the dog rose and trotted out the bedroom door. His nails clicked against the floor's bare wood as he disappeared down the hallway.

"Hey, wait for me." Gingerly, she rose to her

feet. She felt light-headed, but it was nothing like the last time she'd stood and nearly passed out.

A breeze cooled her bare legs and Caleb's scent engulfed her. She remembered then that she only wore Caleb's shirt. The shirttail stretched past her knees and the sleeves hung past her arms. But she felt vulnerable.

Recalling the feel of Caleb's fingers around her arm, she smoothed her hand over the rough cotton sleeve. For an instant, she could almost feel the pressure of his warm skin touching hers.

She squeezed her eyes shut. Stop thinking like this!

Alanna needed to flee this place as quickly as she could. She gazed out the window and watched the windswept branches scrape against the glass panes. Leaving now was impossible.

Frustrated, she pressed her fingertips into her temples. How could she spend another moment alone with him? She took several deep breaths. She could do this. She could do this.

For now she was stuck here with Caleb, but soon—perhaps in a matter of hours—she'd be gone and he'd be nothing but a memory.

"One step at a time, Alanna," she muttered. Step one: clothes. If she were going to stay here, she certainly couldn't run around in Caleb's shirt.

Caleb had said her clothes were ruined, but he

would supply her with others. As promised, on the chest she spotted a neat pile of clothes.

She went to the pile and was grateful to find a thick braided sweater and line-dried wool socks. However, there wasn't a skirt, but a pair of well-worn breeches. She held up the pants. She'd never worn pants before. Lord, but Henry would be horrified.

There'd been a time when she'd have refused to wear anything secondhand, let alone breeches. Women of breeding simply didn't do such things.

But over the last two years she'd watched her finances dwindle to almost nothing. And if diminished circumstances had taught her anything, it had taught her that practicality took precedence over vanity.

Without hesitation, she slipped on the clothes. The breeches felt cold at first and awkward. And not having a corset or, at the very least, a chemise under her sweater felt positively indecent. Still, as her skin warmed the fabric, she had to admit the clothes were comfortable and fit well.

Regaining a measure of control, Alanna moved to the window. Raindrops drizzled down panes of glass smeared with a thick coating of sea salt. Through the film she saw a collection of white-framed buildings that ringed a tall brick lighthouse. The lighthouse looked massive from this vantage point. It stood well over two hundred feet and its granite-and-brick base had to be thirty feet around. Its builders must have used over a million bricks during its construction.

The light atop flashed steady and bright. On for two counts, off for five. The steady beacon signaled that Caleb was on duty.

A sigh dropped her shoulders. Like it or not, having him nearby was comforting.

Her gaze drifted to the yard outside the cottage where the collection of other buildings stood. One building appeared to be a boathouse, another a shed, another a smokehouse. Save for a paltry collection of low-growing cedars by the house, the yard was sandy with sporadic patches of green wiregrass. Sandy dunes blocked her view of the ocean and added to the land's barren, beaten-down appearance.

She spotted Caleb leaving the base of the lighthouse. Dressed in a black jacket, woolen pants tucked into knee-high boots and a stocking cap, he moved with the unconscious confidence of a king. Her face grew hot with the realization that it had been two years since she'd shared his bed. Of course, she'd never be with him in that way ever again. But watching him stride across the yard sent a bolt of electricity down her spine.

There'd been a time when she'd liked to watch

him walk. She'd found his arrogance charming, his overconfidence a sign of strength. Now, she realized both were a sign of weakness, not strength. Arrogance had blinded Caleb to reason and goaded him to take such a dangerous chance two years ago. Good men had died, her father's shipping empire destroyed because Caleb had gambled so boldly.

Caleb unfastened the boathouse door bolt and struggled against the wind to open it. He slipped inside the boathouse and using all his weight, pulled the door closed behind him.

She'd been a fool to come here.

Caleb had been right when he'd said she'd come because of the past. Buried deep in her heart was the hope that he harbored some bit of remorse over what had happened.

But as she had stared into his ice-blue eyes, she'd seen nothing to indicate he harbored any remorse. He'd paid a high price for folly. The world had brought him down a peg or two, but he still had the same overconfidence.

Hot tears burned her eyes. Two years ago, she'd been so in love with him. Despite her father's objections, she had continued to see him. When her father had found out, he'd seemed to relent. He'd offered to throw her the most lavish wedding Richmond had seen. The plans stretched on for weeks and instead of drawing Caleb and her closer, they drove a wedge between them.

The *Intrepid*'s last night in port, she had been filled with an overwhelming need to see Caleb so she'd slipped out of her father's house and in a hired cab, had ridden to the docks. There she'd sneaked aboard his ship and made her way to his cabin. She'd found him, studying his charts and maps.

Her unexpected appearance had surprised Caleb. He'd been busy preparing for his upcoming voyage. But when he'd seen her, he'd known why she'd come.

And as if he, too, were driven, he'd undressed her. They'd made love with an intensity they'd never experienced before. They'd exchanged vows, promising to repeat them in front of a minister when he returned.

The next morning she'd risen before dawn. They both were somber and quiet. As Caleb had seen her to a cab, he'd kissed her.

"I don't like leaving you."

"I'll love you forever and always."

In the following weeks, she'd been ill, and so very tired. And then she'd realized she'd carried his child.

Fear had kept her up at night worrying over the child that would bind them forever. She'd feared her father's reaction. Surely, he'd throw her out of his house. She was certain no one else would go against Obadiah Patterson and offer her shelter. She counted the days until Caleb would return.

Five weeks after Caleb set sail, the weather had turned bad. And then word came of the disaster. And of Caleb's deception.

At first, Alanna didn't believe her father. She'd wanted to travel to Hampton to see Caleb. But when her father presented the evidence against Caleb, she'd realized the man she loved had lied to her. And her heart had shattered.

The day before Caleb's inquest, she'd started to cramp and the bleeding began. Her mind said the miscarriage was a blessing; her heart ached for the child that never would be born.

When Caleb's letters had arrived, she'd been unable to read them. She'd lost her baby, her heart and her life—all because of her foolish attraction for Caleb. She'd given the letters to her father unopened, determined never to think about Caleb again.

Alanna turned from the window. Her hands slid to her flat belly. Tears streamed down her face.

Several minutes passed before she was able to shrug off the sadness and think objectively about her current situation.

The storm prevented her escape now, but that did not mean that she had to remain idle. In the past, she'd found some solace working on her church charity drives. After her father's suicide she'd not been welcome in the church, so she'd made her own baskets for the poor and delivered them alone.

Alanna ventured down the hallway. She passed two closed doors on her right and one on her left before she reached a small parlor. A well-worn braided rug warmed the floor under a settee and two upholstered chairs nestled close to a large potbellied stove, which glowed warm with a fire. In the corner sat a large brass bin that held enough coal to fuel the fire for the next day. Journals, charts and maps were piled high against each wall. A clock hung on the wall. It was five minutes to one.

Functional and efficient, there were no pictures on the walls, knickknacks, or any concession to luxury. The room was Spartan, practical and cold.

She moved through the room to a small kitchen. Toby sat in the corner near a cookstove on a bed made of old quilts, chewing on a bone.

Alanna's stomach growled and the appetite that had escaped her since Caleb's ship had gone down returned with a vengeance. "Got anything for me to eat?"

Toby thumped his tail when he saw her but didn't rise.

Alanna rolled her eyes. "You're a big help."

Steam rose from a kettle atop a cast-iron stove. She leaned close and smelled coffee. She'd have preferred tea. On a roughly hewn table in the center of the small room sat a platter covered with a red-and-white-checkered cloth. Under the cloth, she found cheese and cold meat.

Alanna filled a white porcelain mug with coffee. She sat at the table, savoring the warmth of the mug against her hands. She tasted the coffee. Bitter, but warm. She managed another sip and pinched a piece of cheese and popped it in her mouth. It tasted delicious.

Toby rose and sauntered over to her. He looked up at her with sad eyes. "Oh, so you're hungry now?"

The dog barked.

Alanna pulled off a piece of bread and fed it to the dog. He gobbled it down. For the next few minutes, both ate in companionable silence.

When she was full, she moved back into the parlor and sat on the settee. Toby followed and lay down at her feet. She picked up one of the ledgers in the pile. Its spine read 1866.

Curious, Alanna opened the faded cover and

leafed through the yellowed pages covered with daily entries of Assistant Keeper Roberts.

August 10: Foggy and rainy. Assisted Life Saving Station 2 with rescue of Sally Jane crew. All accounted for. Ship a total loss. Assistant Keeper struck in head by ship's mast. Twenty-three stitches required. No other incidents.

October 1: Breezy. Mild. No vessels spotted. Discovered a steamship in danger waters. Fired Coston Signal. Vessel changed her course.

December 9: Cold. Rain turned to snow. Keeper Pitt died today. Log entry by Assistant Keeper Moore.

Keeper Pitt. Seeing Caleb's surname unsettled Alanna. She rechecked the date on the book's spine. 1866. Twenty years ago. Pitt was a common name, she reminded herself, likely shared with thousands of families. Still, an odd coincidence.

She thought about the businesslike journal entry. *Keeper Pitt died today.* So little a detail, yet her mind spun with unanswered questions. How did he die? Did he have a wife? Children?

She'd already had a taste of how harsh this land

could be out here. No wonder the Assistant Keeper hadn't written more. Time was a luxury he didn't have.

She closed the book. She didn't want to know any more about this place or the men who'd managed it. She wanted to go home.

Alanna went to the steamer trunk behind the settee, hoping to find something more presentable to wear home. To her surprise she found a collection of clothes—a calico dress, a cotton skirt and several pairs of men's breeches. She lifted the wool dress and discovered it had been made for a woman much taller than herself.

Alanna remembered stories Caleb had told her once of the shipwrecks and of the passengers' belongings that often ended up washed ashore.

She laid out the wool dress and inspected its seams. With a needle and thread, she could alter the dress. She held little hope of retrieving her luggage from Crowley, and returning to Richmond dressed as a woman and not a sailor would certainly raise fewer questions.

Alanna dug through the trunk in search of a needle and thread. To her delight, she found a simple tin sewing box outfitted with threads and a small pair of scissors.

Her spirits lifted. Altering the dress would be a small task in the scheme of things. But in her

mind, mending the dress brought her one step
closer to home—and leaving this place behind
forever.

The noon hour had long passed when Caleb left
the lighthouse for home. The storm still raged, a
deadly mix of wind and sea. The savage wind
banged an open shutter against the side of the
cottage. He shoved his hands in his pocket and
lowered his head against the gale, which shoved
him across the lawn toward the house. He was
soaked when he reached the back porch.

He shoved open the door and quickly slammed
it behind him. He paused and tipped his head back
against the door, grateful to be out of the storm.
Lord, but he was so damn tired.

When Alanna's fever had broken last night
he'd returned to the lighthouse to inspect the light.
He'd stayed away most of the day, partly because
there was work to be done and partly because he
didn't want to see Alanna. Seeing her had stirred
too many ghosts from his past.

Still, no matter what his feelings, he could only
avoid her but so long. Until he put her back on a
Virginia-bound coach she was his responsibility.

Sighing, he lit the lantern he kept by the back
door. Its soft halo of light warmed the small en-
tryway as he shrugged off his wet double-breasted

coat and hung it up on a peg. He eased his aching body down to a small bench and pulled off his boots.

Alanna had not changed at all, he thought as he tucked the boots neatly under the bench. Her blond curls still glistened like spun gold and her skin was as smooth as cream. Though she was too thin for his tastes, she was still as stunning as ever.

Self-consciously, he rubbed his fingers over the scar on the side of his face.

When the boiler had exploded on the *Intrepid,* he had been blown free of the boat. But the explosion that had saved his life had also marked him forever with a scar that stretched from his temple down his cheek to his chin. The skin beneath his eye puckered, drawing his left eye down slightly.

Viewed from the right, his face looked as it always had. But from the left, there was no hiding the mark or stopping the questions that followed. When he'd first moved to Easton, the children had been afraid of him. Most of the villagers tried to pretend they didn't see the scar or know about the accident. But often he'd catch someone staring or hear them whispering about him.

Caleb had never considered himself a vain man.

He'd never owned a mirror and he gave only the bare minimum of time to his appearance.

But with Alanna here, he felt self-conscious.

Damn Alanna. She still had the power to turn his life upside down.

Bitterness settled in his heart as he straightened. A thousand times he'd pictured their meeting. In his mind's eye, she'd always been the nervous one—the one off balance. Yet, here he stood worrying over her reaction to him.

Picking up the lantern, he moved into the kitchen where the nutty aroma of coffee greeted him. Puzzled by the fresh smell, he lifted the lid. He'd made coffee last night and expected it to be as thick as tar. But to his surprise, the brew wasn't thick, nor did it smell burned. He gave thanks for the small miracle.

"It's fresh." Alanna's smoky voice startled him.

At the sound of her voice, he stiffened and retreated a step toward the shadows. "You made coffee?"

"Believe it or not, yes."

He found her in her stocking feet, leaning against the doorjamb. Her braided hair draped over her shoulder like a seaman's rope. The pants and sweater he'd left for her accentuated the curve of her hips and the swell of her breasts.

Leaving the clothes had been a practical move, since her clothes were ruined. But he'd never quite expected the prim Miss Patterson to don the rough clothes. Nor had he expected her to look so good in them.

For just a moment, he was transported back to a time when he'd run his hands over those hips. She'd come to him in his cabin, willing and wanting and he'd been unable to refuse what she'd been offering.

Then he'd believed they'd be together forever. He'd wanted nothing more out of his life than to spend time with her. With the small fortune he'd earned, he'd planned to build a house by the sea for them and fill it with their children and laughter.

He tore his gaze from her and poured himself a mug of coffee. "You found the clothes."

"Yes, thank you."

Suddenly, he was very aware of all that he'd lost. Turning away from her, he touched the rough skin of his scars. He tightened his fingers around the mug.

In her stocking feet, she moved into the kitchen toward the stove. She still walked with the straight-backed poise of a queen. Always the queen.

She reached for the coffeepot.

When she'd been ill, he'd been able to be more objective about her. Now she was awake and looking like the Alanna he remembered, his unease grew.

"The coffee's good," he said.

"Thanks," she said, offering a wan smile.

Their relationship had been one of extremes. Fire and ice, never this awkward civility that grated his nerves. He wondered if this was how it was for her and Henry. Was she polite and pleasant or did her blood run hot each time she saw him? "I'm surprised Henry would allow his fiancée in the kitchen with the help."

She glanced up at him, her gaze piercing. The girlishness that had once been in Alanna's eyes had vanished. "I learned to be independent after Father's death and my circumstances were redefined."

"Redefined." His lips curved into a smile. "Only you could make poverty sound noble."

Her voice turned cold. "There wasn't anything noble about it. All our friends abandoned us. We were alone."

"Except for Henry." He hated the stab of jealousy.

Steam rose from her mug. He watched as she stepped back, as if she, too, needed the distance. "I didn't come out here to fight with you. I came out to thank you again for saving my life.'' She hesitated. ''There's a dress in the chest in the parlor. Can I have it?''

He wasn't letting her off the hook that easily. ''Why?''

She pursed her lips. ''I'm altering it. I certainly can't return home looking like this.''

It would be easy to be petty about the dress. He didn't owe her a damn thing. And it would serve her right to return home in breeches and have to explain herself to Henry. ''It's yours.''

His concession seemed to surprise her. When she spoke her tone softened. ''Thank you for all that you've done for me.'' She turned to leave, then stopped. ''If it's worth anything, I'm sorry I came. I should have known that nothing good would come of this visit.''

The unsaid words that had festered in him burned his gut. ''Is that all you regret?''

Anger colored her cheeks and her eyes spit fire. ''What else would you have me apologize for? *I* didn't do anything wrong.''

His fingers bit into his mug. He swore he'd not bring up the past—to acknowledge the past gave it a place of importance it did not deserve. Alanna did not deserve an extra second of his time.

But logic was a poor choice against strong emotions. And before he could stop the words, they tumbled out like bits of broken glass. "Did you bother to read even one of my letters?"

She flinched as if he'd struck her. Her cheeks flushing, she dropped her gaze.

He smacked the cup down on the table. Hot coffee sloshed over his hand. He wanted her to look him straight in the eye. "I loved you, Alanna. I went through hell and back to return to you. I wanted us to be together forever."

His words had her head lifting. Anger had flattened her full lips. She took a step toward him. "I used to believe that until your arrogance ruined us all."

In an instant, he closed the gap between them and grabbed her.

Chapter Six

Alanna gasped as Caleb closed the distance between them. He caught her wrist and pulled her roughly to him until they were nose to nose. His blue eyes blazed bright.

The lantern light shadowed his face, sharpening the edges. Rawboned and dangerous, she thought for an instant, she gazed into the face of the Devil himself.

His hot breath brushed her skin. ''You're right, Alanna. I was arrogant. I believed I could control everything in this world.''

She stared into his eyes, looking for a hint of the man she'd once known. Once they'd been so close she would have sworn they could read each other's thoughts. Together they had been whole, each possessing what the other needed. Now, they were strangers.

"I don't know you anymore."

"I could say the same."

She winced. "You're hurting me."

Caleb released her as if he'd been scorched. He stepped back but the fury had not cooled in his eyes. "Your father got what he wanted after all. We are completely destroyed."

A wiser woman would have backed down, veered from these dangerous waters. A wiser woman would have bided her time until the storm passed and she could escape this madness. But the anger and hurt inside her was a wound that would not heal. "My father had nothing to do with the *Intrepid* sinking. No one is to blame but you. You were the captain."

The muscle in Caleb's jaw pulsed as if he struggled with unnamed emotions. She tensed, waiting for him to fire more irate words.

"You're right." His voice sounded eerily calm. "I am to blame. The ship and her men were *my* responsibility."

The sadness lacing his admission threw her off guard. Pity and concern washed over her. In defense she crossed her arms over her chest and mentally shored up her defenses.

"Until the day I die," he said quietly, "I will regret what happened."

"Then why are you blaming my father?"

His voice grew calm, deadly. "My arrogance contributed to the accident but it didn't sink the *Intrepid,* Alanna."

Coldness spread through her body and settled into her bones. "What are you saying?"

"It was sabotage. Someone rigged the boiler to explode."

Suspicious, she shook her head. "Your men were sloppy. They stored jars of turpentine too close to the boiler."

"Wrong."

"Who would do such a thing?" she challenged.

"Your father."

His answer was so ridiculous, yet her knees started to shake. "You are grasping at straws, Caleb. My father wouldn't sabotage the *Intrepid.* It was the finest ship in his fleet."

Something crossed his face—pain, betrayal, disbelief. "It's true."

Hysterical laughter bubbled inside her. She'd have given her last penny if she could simply wake up from this nightmare. "Really, Caleb, only a coward would pawn off his failings on a dead man."

His fingers curled into tight fists. "I'm no coward. Your father blew up the *Intrepid.*"

Dark fears locked in her heart screamed to be heard. She remembered the Thursday afternoon she'd come home late after a meeting with the grocery. They'd been discussing her past-due bills. The house had been too dark and too quiet, but she'd been so worried over the failing finances, the subtle changes had not registered. She barged into her father's study. She'd found him slumped over his desk, dead, a gun in his hand.

The memory had her stomach jumping. She never knew why her father had killed himself, but it couldn't have been for the reason Caleb was suggesting. "Liar."

A shadow of resentment crossed his eyes before he grabbed her by the arm, picked up the lantern, and started down the hallway.

"Let go of me!" she shouted.

He tightened his hold. "Not until you've learned a thing or two."

Panicked, she stumbled as she tried to keep up with his long strides. "Where are you taking me?"

"Down a peg or two." He dragged her down the hallway as if she weighed nothing more than a sack full of feathers. When he reached the first closed door in the hallway, he opened it and shoved her inside.

She stumbled a step or two before she caught herself. "How dare you!"

Closing the door behind him, he took time to

light another lantern. As the light grew brighter, Alanna could see that she was in his room. A large four-poster bed, with a meticulously smooth white bedspread, dominated the center.

She remembered the last time they'd shared a bed. Lying in his arms had felt so natural, so right. Savagely, she shoved the memory aside.

"I need to get out of this room."

His gaze followed her to the bed. He frowned. "You really don't know me that well at all, do you?"

"Let me go!"

"Not yet, Alanna."

To her surprise, he brushed past her toward a rolltop desk she'd not noticed when she'd come in. As he moved away from her, her heart slowed and she had a chance to study the room. Tall shelves filled with books, a single window that looked out toward the lighthouse, a bureau and a chair by the hearth. Simple, efficient, just like the man.

He pushed back the top, revealing ledgers, maps and books stacked on the desk. He opened a shallow drawer in the center of the desk and pulled out a stack of papers, yellowed and tattered from handling. He flipped through a half-dozen pages before he found the right one.

Turning the page around, he tapped his long tapered finger on a yellowed page. "Read this."

She kept her arms at her side, her gaze on him, but her throat went suddenly dry. "Lies can be written as easily as they are spoken."

His eyes narrowing, his voice deepened. "I was always honest with you. *Admit it.*"

She had never known him to lie. "Perhaps you are more clever than I ever thought."

He jabbed his finger against the page. "You didn't come all this way to give me that damn box. Deep inside you there's doubt. I know why your father shot himself, Alanna."

The tears were quick and hot and they forced her to close her eyes until she could gather her control. "That has nothing to do with this."

"Doesn't it? I think you're the one that's lying now. You're wondering why he'd do such a thing. You are wondering why his fortune evaporated. You're wondering if maybe, just maybe, I'm not the monster he said I was."

She had never spoken of her doubts to anyone, but they plagued her like ghosts. They loomed around her and poisoned her days. "I have no doubts."

"Then you shouldn't have anything to worry about."

Her throat tightened with two years of pent-up

emotion. "Father said the ship sank because you and your men were sloppy and careless."

Caleb nodded. "I took daring risks with the weather, I'll admit to that. But I ran a tight ship. My men were the finest at what they did. But there's a big difference between risk and suicide."

Fear coiled around her heart even as she tried to deny it.

"Look at the ledger," he dared softly.

She slowly lowered her gaze. It was a copy of a bank note. She scanned the document. It stated that her father had taken out a large loan, due the first of August. The amount was staggering. One hundred thousand dollars. A king's ransom!

"This doesn't prove anything. Father may have made poor investment choices but that doesn't make him a saboteur."

"Think back to the last weeks. Your father changed. Admit it."

She thought back to the weeks before the accident. Her father had grown quiet, withdrawn and he'd drunk heavily. His about-face regarding their wedding had been so unexpected. "Father wouldn't sink the *Intrepid*. That ship was the pride of his fleet."

The words struck at unspoken doubts she'd always harbored about her father. When she'd asked him what was the matter, he had fobbed it off. Only after his death did she learn how deeply in debt he truly was.

Caleb took the papers from her and laid them on the desk. He hitched his hip against the side and leaned back, his arms folded over his chest. "Pride was a luxury he could no longer afford. He was broke, Alanna. Sinking the ship and collecting the insurance money was the only way he could survive."

"How did you get these papers?"

His gaze bore into her as if he were trying to read her thoughts. "I came to your house."

Fighting for control, she clenched her fists. "When?"

"Right after the inquest adjourned."

The inquest. It was during those hot listless days that she'd lost the baby. Those were the days she'd lain in her bed, her bedroom curtains closed. "Father never told me that."

He made a sound that might have been a laugh. "I asked to see you, but he said you weren't available to receive me."

The thought that he'd been so close unsettled her. Lord, but she'd needed him then. "That doesn't explain the papers. Father wouldn't have given them to you."

"I doubled back later that night when everyone

was asleep. I broke in.'' He shoved out a sigh. ''I still knew the combination to his safe so it was easy.''

''What would make you suspect Father?''

''I didn't at first.'' His voice grew distant as his mind traveled back to the accident. ''That last night, we were in the middle of the storm. I was on the quarterdeck. The seas were rough but the *Intrepid* was holding together just fine. I knew we'd ride it out. Then one of my men came running up to me. He said there was a fire near the boiler room and the room stank of turpentine. He said before the flames grew too hot he saw shattered glass on the floor and a jar lid.''

''Father said the boiler wasn't maintained properly and your men were sloppy.''

''My men knew their duty. And the boiler was working fine until the fire broke out and we'd not taken on a drop of water at that point.'' He sighed. ''Seconds later, the fire spread and the boiler blew the underside of the ship out. I was blown clear of the ship into the water. I struck my head on something. I'd have drowned if one of my men hadn't dragged me onto a piece of wreckage. They told me later that the ship sank within ten minutes.''

''That doesn't mean Father was to blame.''

''As I said, I didn't suspect him at first. The

events leading up to the accident were hazy and I was wrapped in my own grief.''

''What changed your mind?''

''At the inquest, your father submitted an inventory of the ship's cargo. The instant I read it I knew it was fake. The claim was for five times the actual value. Coincidentally, the payout would have been about one hundred thousand dollars.''

''Fraud,'' she whispered. ''There was never any mention of fraud at the inquest. I would have heard.''

''I didn't say anything.''

''Why?''

''At that point money didn't matter to me. I'd lost my ship and my men. And Obadiah was your father. If he were exposed as a thief there'd have been scandal. I wanted to shield you from all that.''

Caleb had tried to protect her.

''I was willing to let it all go. Then your father produced a mechanic who testified that my crewmen were slack in their duties and that they often stowed flammables in the boiler room.'' He met her gaze. ''I knew he was lying. My men didn't take shortcuts. I told the board. I also told them about the shattered glass and how it would be easy to plant a jar full of the stuff near the boiler.

Once we hit rough seas, the jar would tip and break and then there'd be a fire.''

"It was your word against his."

"Yes. Until an *Intrepid* survivor came forward and testified that your father had been on the ship inspecting the boiler just hours before we sailed."

She felt sick. "Father would have known men would die if he did such a thing."

"At the time I don't think he thought past the money. Later, I suspect his sins caught up to him." A cynical smile touched his lips. "Mistakes have a way of coming back to haunt us."

Her throat dry, she tried to swallow. "He never received any money from the insurance company."

"There was enough doubt for the company to renege on the claim. And his attorney argued there wasn't enough evidence to convict him of murder. The inquest agreed. I knew differently."

She pressed her fingertips to her throbbing temple. "You were the one that was sanctioned."

"A captain who loses his ship is not fit to sail the seas again."

"The sea was your life."

Sadness clouded his eyes. "I was the captain so I was responsible."

"You didn't know."

"I should have been more careful. I should

have added extra inspections. There had to have been something I could have done to prevent the accident.''

Suddenly, she realized the weight he must have borne. A ship of his own had been a dream since he was a child. He'd been abandoned by the world. And her. ''Why break into Father's safe?''

''After you refused to see me, all I had left was duty to my lost men. I owed it to them to discover why your father had done what he'd done. So I broke into his safe.'' He looked tired, drawn suddenly. ''When I saw the note all the pieces fell into place.''

Alanna felt her head spinning. There had to be greater powers at work. She couldn't believe that her world had crumbled because of her father's greed.

Savagely she wiped away a tear.

Silence stretched between them. Outside the rain pelted on the windowpanes and the wind howled. ''Why weren't you there for me at the inquest, Alanna? I needed you sitting behind me.''

She tried to straighten her shoulders, but they felt unbearably heavy. She could have told him about the baby and her illness, but if he knew of this connection they'd shared, she feared he'd never let her go when all she wanted was to flee this place. She wanted to forget about all the heartache and pain and return to the safety of Henry's arms. He would protect her. In Henry's arms, she could forget the past completely.

"It doesn't matter why I wasn't there." She straightened her shoulders. "I should have stayed away as you'd first asked. I will leave you to your lighthouse and your island. Open my father's box or not. I don't care anymore. I will leave you in peace."

Turning, she walked toward the door and reached for the knob.

His deep, raspy voice stopped her. "Do you love Henry?" Bitter resentment tainted his words.

She paused, her hand on the doorknob. "He is a good man and he loves me."

"Do you love him?"

The answer was none of his business, yet for all that she'd done to him, it seemed she owed him as much honesty now as she could muster. "I care for him. And in time, when our children arrive, I know my love will grow."

"You'll grow to hate him in time."

She absorbed his wrath, feeling as if she deserved it. Her body ached. Her mind felt numb. "I failed you, Caleb, but I will not fail Henry. I will be a good wife to him. Our children will be safe and well loved no matter what life brings."

He pushed away from the desk. He closed the distance between them so that he stood right behind her. The heat of his body warmed her cold skin. "And what of the nights, Alanna?"

Her cheeks burned with embarrassment. "Passion is dangerous. The pleasure pales in the face of the destruction."

He reached out to her but she moved away. She feared if he touched her she'd crumble. A part of her wanted to tumble into his arms. There'd been too many times when she'd missed him so much she'd hurt. But she didn't.

Caleb would always take risks. And she needed a man who would be there for her and their children.

"Once you've tasted desire as we have, it is hard to forget. Without desire, your days will be gray and bland."

"I will live without it and be better for it." She would control her inner passions. She would learn to find pleasure in the simple everyday.

"You are like me. A part of you craves the dark and dangerous."

No! She wanted predictability. And she would learn to love Henry. "It's as it should be. We forfeited our chance."

He turned her around so that she faced him. "Then why, even after you failed me, why does it gall me that Henry will be taking the place that should have been *mine*. And that his children will quicken in your belly, not mine.''

''I don't know.'' The simply spoken words slammed into her like a wave. Henry would never take Caleb's place. Alanna knew that now. But he offered no risks. No pain.

Caleb's gaze darkened and his fingers tightened around her shoulders. ''So much wasted. So much lost.''

She swallowed. ''What happened two years ago wasn't my fault.''

''You're right, you didn't rig that boiler to explode. But you also didn't believe in me enough to question the events. You weren't there for me.''

''I will always regret that.''

''Good.'' He strode out of the room.

Chapter Seven

Just past sunrise the next morning, Caleb stood on the crow's nest atop the lighthouse. The rains had stopped temporarily and the warmer air smelled clean and fresh.

In a couple of days the channel would be passable. And Alanna would leave.

Caleb muttered an oath.

Alanna.

Two years ago, twenty-three of his men had died at sea and he'd lost Alanna. He'd borne the crushing pain, accepting it as punishment for his own sins. He'd dared to challenge the elements and had lost.

So, he'd come to the lighthouse, refusing to think beyond the winter season. But winter turned to spring and then summer and he'd stayed on, mostly because he had nowhere else to go.

These last few months he'd come to an uneasy peace about his life. He would never have described himself as a happy man, but there was solace out here near the shoals. Here he made a difference.

There were no investors to satisfy, no one to impress, no complicated social rules to worry over. There was no past and no future. Just today and the sea. And at the end of each day, he knew without question if he'd won or lost.

Alanna's arrival had changed all that.

As he'd stared into her red-rimmed eyes, he'd seen pain that mirrored his own. He'd seen regret, longing and a bone-deep sadness.

Like him, she'd made bad decisions. And like him she had suffered.

He stared down at his hands and realized he was clenching the railing. With an effort he released the wrought iron and settled his focus back on the calming waters.

Restless and edgy, Caleb opened his telescope and scanned the horizon for ships. There'd been none for the last three days, but today there was a schooner. Headed north, she rode low in the water, likely with a cargo from the Caribbean.

A less experienced man would have assumed the storm was finished, but he knew differently. The storm was going to return—likely by nightfall—and it would be just as devastating and deadly as the last. Anyone who ventured out now was at risk.

Caleb shook his head. Her captain was a fool to sail now. No matter how well he thought he knew these waters, the incoming storm could splinter his hull like a twig if he didn't clear the area in time.

Caleb closed his scope and tucked it in his jacket.

Retreating inside, he checked the wicks one last time, then started down the hundred-plus steps that spiraled down the center of the lighthouse.

When he reached the bottom, he wasn't winded. So different than when he'd first arrived here. Weeks in a hospital bed had robbed him of his vigor and climbing the lighthouse stairs had seemed impossible. But he'd been determined to take that first step and then the second. His body had ached and his heart thundered in his chest as his lungs had begged for air.

But he'd made the climb. And with each new day, he'd grown stronger until the stairs were as much a part of him as the wind and sea.

He stared across the compound at the house. The lights were on in the kitchen. He saw Alanna pass in front of a window.

Even now, he could still smell the faint scent

of her perfume and remember how soft her skin was to the touch.

The other night when he'd undressed her. He'd tried to keep his thoughts impersonal but his hands had trembled when his fingers had brushed her skin. He'd been unable to resist touching his fingers to her lips.

She's not yours anymore.

Caleb turned up his collar against the wind and walked the twenty paces to the house. He pushed open the door and a gust of wind swirled around his feet. He closed the door, aware that the house possessed vibrancy with Alanna in it.

He found Alanna standing at the stove, still dressed in her seaman's garb, stirring a kettle of porridge.

Toby looked up from his pallet by the stove. The hound yawned and then laid his head back down.

"Good morning," she said coolly.

"Morning."

He sat down on the bench to pull off a boot, noting that the large seaman's sweater she wore accentuated the elegant length of her neck and the swell of her full breasts. Her long wheat-colored curls, tied back with a length of rope, brushed the top of her hips. Her breeches clearly outlined her figure. Suddenly the pants seemed too tight.

He'd kissed that neck.

Suckled those breasts.

Savagely, he wondered if Henry had done the same.

Caleb shoved his hand through his hair and turned away. Stow those thoughts. His eyes were set ahead on the horizon now.

He jerked off wet boots, placed them neatly under the bench then shrugged off his jacket and hung it on its assigned peg.

"The weather's clearing," Alanna said. She sounded overly formal, a tone she always took when she was upset.

"Aye, it's clearing, but there's more weather behind it."

"But we can make the mainland if we leave now."

"We might, but there won't be time enough for me to get back to the lighthouse. And someone has to be here to man the light."

She wanted to get angry, he could see that, but she held her emotions in check. "When can I leave?"

"A day or two."

"That long?" Her shoulders sagged. "The mainland is so close."

"In this weather, the mile-long trip might as

well be a thousand miles. You know better than most that these waters are dangerous, Alanna.''

"I'd almost be willing to take the risk.''

He rose and moved toward the stove. He picked up the hot pot of simmering coffee and poured himself a cup. Cold and tired, he was grateful he didn't have to wait the hour brewing time. "Impulsive as ever, Alanna.''

Fire sparked in her eyes. "I am not impulsive.''

Caleb had seen that look before. They'd had their share of arguments in the past. Her spirit had always warmed his blood. "If you're looking for a fight today, Alanna, I'll give it to you. I'm in no mood to deal with a spoiled woman.''

Her chest rose and fell as she stared at him. "I want to get off this island and start living my life. I don't see what's so selfish about that!''

"I won't get myself killed so you can run home to Henry.'' He sipped his coffee.

"This isn't about Henry,'' she snapped.

He sat down at the table. He'd rather have her spitting mad than indifferent. "How long have you two been separated? Four or five days?''

"Seven.''

"By tomorrow he'll realize you aren't at home. He's going to figure out you came here and he's going to hate it.''

Defiance straightened her slender shoulders. "He'll understand when I explain."

"Will he?"

She glared at him. "I'm not worried about Henry. He loves me."

The bit of desperation in her voice had him raising his head. When she got a full view of his scars in daylight, she flinched and dipped her gaze. Irritated by her reaction, he felt an unreasonable need to punish. "Henry always wanted what was mine."

Fire flashed in her eyes. "I haven't been *yours* for a very long time." She lifted her chin. "And if you'll remember, I knew Henry long before I met you."

Caleb's jaw tensed. "A fact he always enjoyed pointing out to me."

Born into old money, Henry had fully expected to marry Alanna and take over Patterson Shipping. And likely, he'd have done just that if Caleb hadn't moved to Richmond. Hungry to make his fortune, Caleb had worked harder than three men and he quickly caught the notice of Obadiah Patterson. He'd risen through the company fast, and if that weren't sin enough in Henry's mind, he'd captured Alanna's heart. Henry hated Caleb, and he'd told him every chance he'd had, though he was careful to hide his feelings from Obadiah and Alanna.

Alanna shoved out a sigh, as if she were suddenly weary. "I've no energy to cover old ground. What's done is done. Let it go."

Let it go. Alanna made it sound easy. After all the pain and misery, letting her go should have been simple. But it wasn't.

Alanna moved to the window over the sink and gazed out. "It isn't raining now. Is it safe to go for a walk?"

"It's cold out there."

Taking his statement as a *yes,* she moved to the back door. "The cold won't bother me as long as the air is fresh."

Unlike the young misses in her social set, Alanna had never been content to spend endless hours inside. Keeping her inside now would be futile.

"Stay clear of the surf," he warned. "They've a fierce pull in them today."

She reached for a spare coat of his hanging on a peg by the back door. "Yes. Yes, I know. I shan't be gone long."

She shrugged on the coat, which seemed to swallow up her small frame, and then whistled for the dog. Toby's ears perked and he rose quickly.

The dog hurried toward her. She scratched him between the ears and the two went outside.

Caleb didn't rise from his seat at the table until she and Toby were gone. Only then did he walk to the back door. He watched Alanna and Toby walk across the wind-blown yard toward the dunes. She picked up a pinecone and tossed it hard. Toby ran after the cone, his tail wagging.

"Damn dog," Caleb muttered. "Acts like she hasn't been gone at all."

Alanna's hips swayed as she followed the dog past the lighthouse toward the beach. She paused on the dune, picked a handful of sea oats, and then disappeared toward the beach.

"Impulsive as ever," he muttered.

Caleb finished his coffee and put his mug in the sink. He noticed then that the dishes he'd left soaking the last few days had been cleaned and put away. The countertops had been wiped and the floor swept.

The old Alanna wouldn't have bothered to clean or straighten. She'd have worried over her hair or lost herself in the latest copy of *Harper's*.

There were other changes in her. She didn't laugh freely like she used to. She was more direct and she hadn't tried to win him over with flattery. Thinner than he remembered, her cheeks had sharpened and her eyes looked more deep-set. Her hands were callused now.

But she still was impulsive.

And she'd not been there for him the one time he'd really needed her.

He needed sleep. He didn't need to spend precious energy thinking about Alanna.

Still, the surf was rough today. If she were to see a shell or if the dog chased a gull into the water, she wouldn't think twice about running into the waves.

The *ifs* hitched in his gut. And before he thought, he'd pulled on his boots and coat.

Alanna sat on the beach, staring at the vast ocean. In the distance a slim patch of blue sky sliced through thick dark clouds. Though the morning sun streamed through the break in the clouds, she could see it would soon be chocked out by more bad weather.

Still, just sitting here on the beach invigorated her.

It had been two years since she'd been to the beach. There'd been nights after her father had died when she'd lain awake dreaming of the hot sun and the crashing of the waves. Memories had sustained her.

Toby ran into the surf, chasing seagulls, barking. Wind rustled through the sea oats and stirred the salty ocean scents.

Last night after Caleb had left for his shift, she'd sneaked back into his study and reread the bank notes her father had signed two years ago. She'd stared at his bold signature, trying to find some reason that would prove Caleb wrong. But the longer she sat and stared, the more she had believed Caleb. In the end, she left the box her father had bequeathed him and closed the door on her way out.

She buried her face in her hands. Tears filled her eyes. So much loss.

"That dog is going to drown." Caleb's raspy voice sounded behind her.

Tipping her head back, she dashed a tear from her face. "He loves to run."

Caleb stood next to her, staring toward the waves and his dog. "He doesn't have the sense to know there's a riptide out there."

Caleb whistled and Toby's ears perked. The dog bounded back through the waves toward his master, barking all the way.

Laughing, Caleb picked up a piece of driftwood and tossed it down the beach.

Alanna had a clear view of his profile and allowed herself a moment to study him. The sun had added a few crinkles around his eyes, deepened the lines around his mouth, but both made him more attractive, if that were possible.

She cleared her throat, trying to steady her emotions. All night, she'd been surrounded by his possessions. A weathered blue shirt, charts with his bold handwriting on them, the mug he drank from—all reminders of the man.

They'd shared so much yet she didn't know how to talk to him. She truly did not want to spar with him anymore. Little time remained before she left the island and never saw him again. "You must be exhausted," she said.

He squatted beside her, his hands clasped together and draped over his knees. He scooped up a handful of sand and let it trickle from his fist. "I'll get some sleep soon enough."

She kept her voice light. "It's hard to believe there is more bad weather coming."

He shrugged. "Warm sunny days are just as common as cold rainy ones these last days in May."

She picked up a handful of sand and let it filter through her fingers. "You're right. I'd forgotten." The weather in Richmond was much like the coast. They'd picnicked on the beach in early May once. The sun had been hot, the breeze soft and they'd lain on a quilt for hours talking about their future. They'd even named their first child. Adam if it was a boy. Elizabeth if it was a girl.

"It's been two years since I've been to the ocean," she managed to say.

He rubbed his hand over his face. "I doubt I could sleep without the sounds and smells." He kept his face turned partly away, his emotions hidden. "Why'd you stay away from the ocean? You always loved it."

"After Father lost his company, he couldn't bear the sight of the ocean. We never left Richmond again. He spent nearly a month locked in his room with the curtains drawn. And then he died."

The lines in his forehead deepened. "Did he ever give a reason why he killed himself?"

"I thought he was despondent over the accident. Now I realize it was much more." It was her way of saying that she believed him.

He stared at her a long moment then shifted his gaze to the ocean. A heavy silence settled between them.

Her gaze skimmed from the light past the barren dunes to the bleak horizon. "Why would you come to such a place? It's the end of the earth."

Caleb shoved out a breath. "Exactly what I was looking for."

Guilt blew through Alanna like a cold wind.

She knew from friends that Caleb had been ostracized from society and the shipping business. No one would speak to him, let alone hire him.

"I met a man in town. His name is Sloan. He seems protective of you."

"I saved his nephew when his boat turned over in the sound."

"Do you see people from the village often?"

"Every few weeks."

"You must get lonely."

Though Caleb was but inches from her, he felt a million miles away. "It's part of the job."

She wanted to tell him she was sorry. But the words sounded so paltry, and they died in her throat. She'd shared all her hopes and fears with this man once, yet she'd never felt more alone in her life.

The isolation grew unbearable. Alanna reached her hand out to Caleb. She laid her hand over his. He tensed but did not move.

She turned his palm over and studied his hands, rough from the cold and wind. Strength and raw power radiated from them. His lifeline stretched across his palm. An old soul, an aged gypsy sailor had said about Caleb once.

"These last few days have been harder than the last two years," she said.

He stiffened, but didn't speak. She felt his pulse thud harder against the tender skin of his wrist.

"Hating you was simple and pure," she whispered. "It was black and white, no room for pain. But I can't hate you anymore. I don't want us to be enemies." Unshed tears burned the back of her throat.

He pulled his hand away from hers and laid it on her shoulder. Through the fabric she could feel the warmth of his skin. "You want me to be your *friend?*"

"You make it sound so awful."

He laughed as if he were teetering on insanity. "I can't wish you good fortune and watch as you marry another."

"Why not?" Liquid flames shot through her veins, making her dizzy.

"Because my thoughts are not the least bit friendly toward you." His gaze pinned her. "Every time I look at you I want to strip you down naked and make love to you."

Chapter Eight

Shocked by his earthy language, she jumped to her feet. She opened her mouth to speak, but couldn't form any words. Heat flooded her body.

"You're going to catch a fly," Caleb said easily.

She snapped her mouth closed. Finally, stumbling, she sputtered, "You're not serious."

Caleb rose and calmly brushed the sand from his hand. His gaze trapped her. "I'd make love to you right now on this beach if you gave me the word."

His raspy voice ignited scorching memories of their last night together—his lovemaking, the erotic words he'd whispered in her ear, and the way her body enveloped him when he entered her.

She'd spent the last two years telling herself that the passion she'd shared with Caleb hadn't been as intense as she'd remembered. She'd come to believe that her memories had gotten tangled and distorted by time and loneliness.

That kind of desire didn't exist between a husband and wife. Her parents had certainly never felt that way about each other. Their relationship had been cordial, polite, if not a little distant. When her mother had died of a kidney disease, her father had gotten on with his life without difficulty.

Now, the desires she'd worked so hard to forget came roaring to life. They raged inside of her.

"I—I don't think that kind of talk is appropriate given our circumstances," she whispered.

He shoved his hands in his pockets and leaned so close to her she could see the shards of blue in his eyes. "Just being honest, *friend.*"

"You're making fun of me. Friends don't speak to each other like that."

He feigned innocence. "That's how I speak to my friends."

"Well, I'm not one of your *male* friends."

"Exactly."

Alanna raised her hand to her racing heart and stepped back. The passion they'd shared had nearly ruined her two years ago. She would not give in to it. She would not!

She struggled to catch her breath. "I won't sleep with you again."

His white teeth flashed. "I wasn't talking about sleep."

Flustered, she shook her head. "There you go playing with words again. You know what I mean. I'm not going to do *that* with you again."

He circled behind her, yet remained close. His chest skimmed her back. "Aren't you a little curious?"

Her mouth felt dry. "About what?"

"If *that* is still as good as it was before." He circled around, his gaze reminding her of a shark as he hovered close before a kill.

"I don't think about those nights." In truth, she had remembered every time he'd touched her, but exploring the memory was like sailing into dangerous waters.

Cold blue eyes narrowed in speculation. "Sure you do. You think about it every time you undress. Every time you slip into a hot tub. Every time you are alone. You remember what it feels like to have my hands on you."

A violent wave of heat shot through her. "I don't!"

He cocked an eyebrow. "And you know what else? You're wondering if you can live with

Henry and a lifetime of his lukewarm lovemaking.''

She wiped her palms against her pants leg. When Henry kissed her she felt nothing. *Nothing*. Unless she allowed memories of Caleb to drift into her mind. ''That's not true,'' she whispered.

A half smile tugged at the corner of his lips as if he knew he'd struck a nerve. ''I'll bet his kisses are polite, neat. He doesn't muss your hair. He doesn't leave your lips feeling bruised. Your heart beating fast.''

She squeezed her eyes shut. ''Real love is deeper than just passion. Real love is born of respect and kindness.'' These were the emotions she felt when she thought of Henry. Her thoughts tumbled in her head. ''I love Henry.'' The words sounded forced, as if she were trying to convince herself as much as him.

He laid his hands on her shoulders. Opening her eyes, she jumped as if she'd been shocked. ''If you came to my bed, I'd muss your hair. Your heart would slam in your chest. And every muscle in your body would know that I'd made love to you.''

For just the briefest moment, she let herself imagine what it would feel like to have him inside her again. She imagined his naked chest brushing against hers. His lips kissing her. A delicious ache spread through her body.

Alanna froze. Good Lord, what was she doing? This was wrong. Caleb steered her toward dangerous waters again.

Henry had never made her feel like this. He'd never made her *want* so. And wanting was so dangerous. It turned the wise into fools. It made the sane crazy. Still the wanting thrummed in her veins like an opiate.

"You want me," he whispered.

"This isn't what love is about." Unable to resist, Alanna raised her finger to touch his scarred face. It felt rough, marred. The face she'd touched a thousand times felt nothing like she remembered.

Tension radiated through his body, as if he'd read her thoughts. The pain and the loss they'd endured returned and overshadowed the moment.

His lips twisted into a cynical smile. "You keep talking about love. I'm not talking about love. I'm talking about sex."

She should have left right then and there and returned to the cottage. But she didn't. "You can't have one without the other."

Desire still burned in his eyes. "I can assure you that it's very possible. We can go back to my room now and I'll show you."

His crude words hit their mark. She heard his message loud and clear. He wanted her, but he didn't love her.

Tightness banded her chest and she felt as if all the air were being squeezed from her lungs. Unshed tears burned at the back of her throat. It shouldn't matter that he didn't love her anymore.

But it did.

Hours later as Caleb had predicted, another storm swept over the Outer Banks with violent force. However, Alanna was oblivious to the high winds and pelting rain. She'd done her best to keep busy. First she'd pulled vegetables and meat from the larder and started a stew. She'd only learned to cook last fall—when finances had forced her to let her cook go. But she discovered that cooking could be a pleasant escape. Though her meals weren't fancy, they were hearty and tasty.

Then, she'd cleaned the pantry, scrubbing the shelves until her hands were numb and her back ached. But no matter how hard she couldn't wrestle free of the sadness that had settled in her bones.

Caleb didn't love her.

She sat in the parlor next to the hearth where a fire blazed. Draped over her lap was the castoff dress she'd found in the trunk earlier. Scissors in hand, she worked at undoing the garment's bodice seams. She'd wear the dress home, but after that, she never wanted to see it again. She wanted to forget every moment she'd spent here.

Alanna would give everything she owned if she could turn the clock back. She'd have lived her life so differently two years ago if given the chance. She'd have read his letters. She'd have found the strength after her miscarriage to go to him and tell him about the baby so they could have mourned together.

Caleb didn't love her.

So many mistakes, so many things had gone wrong. Knowing the past was unfixable tore at her heart.

A gust of wind knocked a branch against the window. Alanna started and pricked her finger with the needle. Annoyed, she sucked the tip of her injured pinkie as she looked up at the window.

She set her sewing aside and walked to the window. When was this storm going to end? She wanted so desperately to leave.

Lantern light flashed near the boathouse. Through the rain and wind she saw Caleb, wrestling the boathouse door closed. Once he'd secured the door and held the lantern high, she could see that he'd pulled out a dory on a low-lying wheeled cart. He tied the lantern to the end of the boat and started to drag the trailer over a rutted path that cut through the dune.

She stared up at the gray-black sky. What was he up to? "Dear Lord, he can't be going out into the ocean."

Caleb guided the boat closer to the dune. No man in his right mind would attempt the seas in a storm like this alone.

Except Caleb.

Her reaction was instinctual and she didn't question it. She had to help him.

She grabbed her coat and pulled on a stocking hat. Tucking her head low, she ran into the rain across the yard toward Caleb. She caught up to him at the base of the dune. Staring at the boat, she marveled at the incredible strength required to pull it this far. "Where are you going?"

He didn't spare her a glance as the rain pelted his face. "Go back inside, Alanna."

She stared at his grim features. "You are not going out into the ocean."

He stopped and pointed toward the ocean. Rain dripped from his face. "Look."

Her gaze followed his outstretched hand toward the sea. A small schooner had run aground. It listed on its right side. Torn white sails flapped in the wind. On the deck of the ship stood four figures, clinging to the cracked mast. "Oh my God! When did that happen?"

"They've been skimming the coast for a couple of hours. I shot off warning flares but they didn't see them. They ran aground a half hour ago."

The day she'd nearly drowned the water had been so cold. "What's going to happen to them?"

He wrapped the boat rope around his gloved hand and started toward the water. Blankets were piled two deep in the bottom of the boat. "If I don't get them off that boat soon, they'll go down with the ship."

She glanced up at the churning seas and her stomach rolled. Memories flashed of falling into the water and of her lungs aching for water. Her hands began to sweat. The schooner's dark hull shifted in the surf. Shouts of the victims reached the beach.

She ran to the other side of the boat and grabbed hold of the boat's rim. "I don't know anything about rescues."

"Go back inside, Alanna. This is dangerous work," he shouted over the wind and rain. "I've got my hands full as is and I don't need to be worrying about you."

Alanna didn't move. "We're wasting time."

Caleb glanced toward the ship beyond the dunes and back at the tight set of Alanna's mouth.

He better than anyone understood just how stubborn she could be. "Just help me get the boat into the water."

Nodding, she forced her fingers to bite into the boat's rim as she pulled in time with Caleb. It took all her strength and his to pull the boat over the dune and down through the soft sand to the water's edge. Icy surf roared up the beach, splashing against her legs and seeping into her boots.

Caleb seemed oblivious to the cold as he locked the oars in the oarlocks. "When we get the boat past the breakers, I'll jump in," he shouted over the wind. "You get back on shore and wait for me."

Grim-faced, Alanna nodded. She had no intention of leaving him, but understood this was not the time to share her thought with Caleb. He'd only argue and that would slow them down.

Caleb waited until the waves were dashing back to the ocean before he shouted, "Push!"

Alanna obeyed.

The pull of the surf tugged the boat toward the spot where the waves broke. As the boat rolled over the waist-high waves, Caleb swung himself into the boat.

"Go back to shore!" he shouted.

Alanna gripped the side of the boat. "I'm coming with you."

"Alanna, I don't have time to argue," he shouted.

"Then don't. Pull me aboard." Her fingers were cold and her teeth chattered, but she swung her leg up and over the side of the boat. She tried not to think too much about what could go wrong.

Caleb swore as he grabbed her by the coat collar and hauled her into the boat. She tumbled headfirst onto the boat's hard bottom.

With as much dignity as she could muster, she righted herself and faced Caleb who sat with his back to the ocean. Wordlessly, he glared at her as he started to pump the oars with his powerful arms. He strained against the tide until the current took hold of the boat and yanked her out to sea toward the schooner.

A wave crashed against the bow. Alanna swallowed a scream and stiffened her shoulders. "I'm okay. I can do this!"

"Steady," Caleb said. "We'll be just fine," he said without a trace of worry.

Alanna curled her trembling fingers into fists. She could do this. She could! Caleb was close. He was in charge. Everything would be fine.

Oh God, oh God. How had she gotten herself into this?

Caleb set his course, giving her a full view of the jagged scar on his face. It was a reminder of how she'd failed him. She would not let him down this time.

As Caleb had said, the schooner was sinking, its hull cracked by a shoal. As they moved closer, she could make out the figure of a woman clinging to the mast. Next to her stood three men—two dressed as seamen, the other in a suit. Each wore the same tight masks of fear.

"Hello there!" Caleb shouted as he maneuvered the lifeboat closer to the schooner. "Alanna, take the oars."

Alanna scooted forward and slipped into Caleb's spot as he moved toward the front of the boat. She had to adjust her grip a couple of times before she felt as though she had a good hold. Keeping the boat steady was far trickier than she'd thought. Caleb had made it look easy.

Like a cat, Caleb moved to the front of the dory with a thick circle of rope around his arm. He tied one end to his boat and then tossed the other end to the men on the wreck. "Pull us alongside of your vessel. When it's secure we'll start taking people on."

A young seaman tied the rope off. "Yes, sir!"

Soon the lifeboat was moored alongside the listing schooner. Alanna secured the oars then reached for the first blanket.

Caleb stared up at the young sailors. He

frowned as if he recognized the boys. "Where's your captain?" Caleb shouted.

The young seaman's face turned crimson. "Washed overboard with two other crewmen. We are all that is left."

Caleb seemed to take in what the seaman said, but made no comment. "The woman first."

The woman was young, not much older than Alanna. Tension tightened her lips. Her soft brown hair was tied at the nape of her neck and her skin was so pale. Her full, wet skirts and cape flapped in the wind as she held on to her bundle.

Balancing one foot on the rowboat and the other against the schooner, Caleb held out his hand to the woman.

She let loose of the mast and took Caleb's hand, but refused to let go of her bundle.

"Drop the package," Caleb shouted.

"It's all we have left," the woman wailed.

Her white-knuckle grip and strained face showed just how scared she was.

"You won't live long enough to enjoy anything if you don't let go of the package. Let it go," Caleb commanded.

The man dressed in a suit clung to the ship's ropes. "For God's sake, Debra, let it go."

"It's our silver," she shouted.

"Let it go," the man repeated.

The woman hesitated then reluctantly let the package fall into the water. It floated on the surface for only a second before it sank under the waves.

"Take my hand!" Caleb said.

Saying a prayer, Debra stepped one foot onto the boat. The rise and fall of the waves shifted the surf bow and the woman froze. "I'm going to die!"

The man dressed in the suit panicked and pulled Debra back onto the schooner. The sudden movement threw Caleb off balance and he tipped forward.

Alanna jumped up and grabbed hold of his coattail. She dug her heels into the boat bottom and steadied him.

The extra bit of help was all Caleb needed to regain his footing. He glanced down at Alanna and nodded his thanks.

"I can't do it," Debra shouted.

"My wife's expecting a baby," her husband said. "This is too much for her."

Ignoring the man, Caleb reached out for Debra again. He shifted his weight to accommodate the boat's movement. The woman started to cry.

Caleb locked gazes with the woman. "Give me your hand. I won't let you die." His voice was so calm, Alanna would have thought they were all standing on dry land and it was a sunny mild day in June. "Do it for your child."

The fear faded in the woman's eyes a fraction and she lifted her chin. She glanced back at her husband and drew in a breath. She took Caleb's hand.

Caleb smiled. "That's it. Now take two steps and it'll be over."

In one quick motion, she stepped onto the boat. She staggered forward under the weight of her skirts before she collapsed down to the seat in front of Alanna. Shaking badly, the woman wrapped her arms around her chest.

Alanna draped a large warm blanket around the woman. "You're safe now. Just rest."

The woman nodded. "God bless you." Fat tears rolled down her face.

Caleb's focus shifted back to the schooner and this time he helped the first seaman on board. The young man's long lanky body folded into a C-shape as he tried to shake off the cold.

Alanna wrapped a blanket around the young man. "That'll help."

The look of sheer gratitude in the boy's face tugged at her heart. "Bless you, ma'am."

The man dressed in the suit was next. He stumbled as he stepped onto the bow. Caleb steadied him, guiding him to the seat next to the woman.

The man leaned toward his wife and kissed her on her forehead. "Thank God you are all right, Debra. The baby?"

Debra smiled as tears streamed down her face. "He's fine, Thomas. He keeps kicking me."

The husband looked toward the schooner. "I fear we'll lose everything. But we are alive and that is all that matters."

Debra touched her husband's cheek. "I'm sorry I dropped the package. It had all our silver in it. We are penniless. What are we going to do now, Thomas?"

Thomas cupped his wife's face. "That doesn't matter, Debra. You are alive. The baby is fine. That's all that matters. The rest will work itself out."

Tears streamed down Debra's face as she kissed her husband.

Their foreheads touching, the couple closed their eyes and whispered words of love to each other.

The couple's closeness moved Alanna. Theirs was the kind of love she'd dreamed of—the kind her parents had not shared; the kind she prayed she and Henry would find; the kind she'd once shared with Caleb.

Chapter Nine

Within minutes, the last man was in the dory. Alanna moved to the back of the boat as Caleb settled into position between the oars. When he gave the sign, the last seaman untied the boat from the schooner and pushed them away from the wreck toward shore.

With the two young seamen's help, Caleb easily steered the boat to shore. Alanna said a prayer of thanks when she heard the flat-bottom boat bottom skim against the sandy shore.

With the danger past, exhaustion overtook Alanna's body. She wanted nothing more than to drag herself back to the cottage and collapse into bed.

Instead, she pulled her cold, wet body up and helped Debra over the side and through the surf up to the beach. The woman dropped to the sand beside Alanna.

Debra could barely lift her head. "Land never felt so good."

Alanna glanced over her shoulder and watched as Caleb and the three men dragged the boat ashore. When the boat was secured out of the tide's reach, they flipped it upside down.

As Alanna watched Caleb walk up the beach, with his broad shoulders straight, she felt a swell of pride. If not for him, these people would have perished.

Caleb lifted his gaze and met hers. He stared at her an extra beat and she could feel the heat rising in her body.

Her throat tightened with emotions she had thought long dead. She dropped her gaze and wrapped her arms around Debra's shoulders. "If you can stand, I'll guide you to the cottage. There's warm clothes and food waiting for you there."

Debra nodded. "Music to my ears. Now all I have to do is find the strength to stand."

Thomas reached them at that moment. He wrapped his arm around Debra's shoulders. "I'll carry you."

Debra stood but wouldn't allow him to lift her into his arms. "I can walk."

"The cottage is just over the dunes," Alanna said. The sailors moved toward her and she motioned them in her direction. They all followed her across the sand over the dune toward the cottage.

The wind had grown stronger and the rain felt like cold daggers by the time she wrestled the back door of the cottage open. Yet, there was deep satisfaction taking root in her bones. For the first time in her life, she felt as if she'd done something of great importance.

Her spirits lifting, she shrugged off her coat and hung it on a peg. Lighting a lantern, she moved to the kitchen stove. She guided her charges to the kitchen table.

Alanna stoked the fire and tossed kindling into the burning embers. "Take a seat at the table. Just give me a minute and I'll heat up the stove. I've coffee to warm your bones and a fresh pot of stew."

Thomas pulled his chair close to Debra's. He took her cold hand in his and rubbed it to make her feel warmer. "God bless you, ma'am."

Up close, the sailors looked younger—boys really. One was tall and lean with short curly brown hair. He wore spectacles. The other sailor had dirty-blond hair, a round face and a handful of freckles sprinkled over his nose. They huddled under their blankets, shivering.

Alanna pulled four coffee mugs down from the

shelf above the stove and poured each person a cup. Then she served them bowls of stew. She mentally catalogued the supplies she'd seen in the pantry. "I've bread, too."

Caleb was the last inside. He shrugged off his coat and boots and moved into the kitchen. He stopped for a moment and simply stared as if he couldn't quite believe what he saw. "Stew? Where'd that come from?"

She felt awkward, as if she had somehow overstepped. "I made it earlier."

His gaze lingered and for just a moment she imagined his attitude softened toward her. "Thanks. A hot meal is a rare treat."

The smooth rich tone of his voice had her transfixed. She'd forget about the others and God help her, Henry. It was just the two of them.

He didn't move, as if he'd felt the same pull. She remembered how good it had been between them once. How much they'd laughed. It hadn't been all bad times.

With some effort, Caleb tore his gaze from her and shifted it to the others. "There are dry clothes in the back room," he said, his voice rough. "Once you've eaten, I'll show everyone the way."

One of the young sailors clinked his spoon

against the bottom of his bowl. "I reckon that was the best I ever ate."

Thomas nodded. "Excellent fare."

Alanna turned from Caleb to those she'd helped rescue. "I've got plenty."

Caleb moved into the room. Immediately, Thomas started to rise, but Caleb motioned him back into his seat. "Sit. Eat."

"We can't thank you enough, sir," Thomas said.

"Glad to be of help."

Alanna pushed a mug of hot coffee in Caleb's hands. Her fingers brushed his icy flesh. "Are you hungry?"

He held the mug close, staring at her through the rising steam. "Yes."

She smiled. "Let me make you a plate."

He slid into a chair. Exhausted and weather-beaten as he was, she'd never remembered a time when he was more attractive.

Caleb started to eat. "This is good."

Alanna chuckled and muttered, "You sound surprised."

"I am."

Debra took Alanna's hand and squeezed it. "I haven't even asked your name."

Alanna forced her focus to the young woman. "Alanna."

Tears streamed down the young woman's face. "God bless you, Alanna."

Thomas wrapped his arm around his wife. "We'll always be in your debt, Mr...."

Caleb took the younger man's hand. "Pitt. Caleb Pitt."

As if sensing their thoughts, Caleb shifted his gaze to the young sailors. "I thought you two were in Savannah."

The sailors glanced up at Caleb, but remained silent, huddled under their blankets. They seemed to want to melt into the floorboards.

The boy with blond hair blushed. "We were. But we were able to get work on a ship bound to Richmond."

Caleb's gaze darkened. "You know better than to travel in this kind of weather, Alex."

Alex shrugged. "The skipper said we could beat the storm."

Caleb frowned. "Who was your captain?"

"Jamison," the other boy said.

Caleb snorted. "You should have known better, Ryan. I told you a month ago not to sail with him."

Alanna watched the exchange. Caleb treated them as if he were their father, which of course he wasn't. "You know these boys?"

Caleb nodded. "From town."

She supposed as lightkeeper, he knew most of the people on the coast. "Don't be too hard on them. They've been through a lot."

"Caleb, we thought we could beat the storm," Ryan said.

Caleb sipped his coffee. "Ryan, you know as well as anyone that Jamison will do most anything for a profit."

Thomas set down his cup. "To the boys' credit, they did try to talk the captain out of sailing. But I was so eager to get Debra to Richmond and I didn't heed their advice."

The smile on Alanna's face froze. "Richmond? What takes you there?" It was a small town and it would be just a matter of time before she ran into them again.

Thomas straightened his shoulders. "I've been given a parish there. St. Matthews."

Alanna cleared her throat. "St. Matthews?"

Thomas cocked his head. "Do you know it?"

The church wasn't hers but she knew enough people who attended it. Panic exploded inside her. If word were to get back to Henry, he'd be furious. "Yes, I do as a matter of fact."

Debra's face brightened. "You've been to Richmond?"

Her knees felt as if they would buckle. She

could feel Caleb's gaze on her as she struggled to think of something to say. "Yes."

"Do you get back often? I would so love to have you visit us when you do," Debra said.

"That's very kind of you." Alanna felt sick.

Abruptly, Debra pressed her hand to her stomach. "Oh my, that was a hard kick."

Thomas's face whitened. He looked at Alanna. "I don't want to be more bother, but is there a room where we could lie down?"

Caleb was the one who answered. "I've rooms for everyone. If you'll just follow me."

Debra smiled. "Thank you again, Mr. Pitt and you, too, Mrs. Pitt."

Mrs. Pitt!

Alanna felt as if the floor rolled under her feet. Her mouth open, she looked at Debra, not sure if she should correct the woman or not. Her gaze met Caleb's. He frowned and for a moment she thought he'd correct Debra. If he did, Henry would be furious and what remained of her good name in Richmond would be destroyed.

"We were happy to help," Caleb said.

Alanna released the breath she was holding. "I'll just clean up the kitchen."

Ryan looked up from his bowl. "Ma didn't say anything about you getting married, Caleb."

Alanna froze.

Caleb shrugged. "I haven't had much time to visit with the family."

Alex shook his head. "News like that would spread like a hurricane."

Alanna ducked her head, trying not to meet the boy's face. This was all getting too complicated, too fast.

Ryan snapped his fingers. "Did you two marry last month when you sailed to Virginia, Caleb?"

"That's about right," Caleb said.

Alanna stared at Caleb, her expression puzzled by the news of his trip. She itched to ask him about it but didn't, knowing it would expose the lie.

"Best get out of those wet clothes soon, Alanna," Caleb said. "You'll get sick again if you don't."

He almost sounded like a solicitous husband. To her chagrin, she liked it. "I'm fine."

He sighed. "For once, just listen to me."

She glanced at the dirty dishes. "I really should clean up first. But—"

"A *good wife* listens to her husband."

She swallowed her argument, not wanting to cause a fuss with everyone listening so closely. She followed Caleb down the hallway. He paused in front of the larger of the rooms and assigned it to the Randalls. The next room was smaller but fit for the two seamen.

Alanna started to move past Caleb and retire to the room that had been hers since her arrival.

Caleb cleared his throat. "Mrs. Pitt?"

She froze. "Yes?"

He opened the door to his room, the one room she'd been careful to stay clear of since last night. His eyes danced with challenge. "You've walked right past our room, dear."

"I'm sorry?" Her mother had taught her when she was a child that if you didn't like a question it was best to pretend you hadn't heard it. Most gentlemen caught the hint that they'd breached etiquette and rarely dared repeat the question.

Caleb pushed his door open wide, grinning at Thomas who had paused in his doorway. "We just rearranged the living quarters and *Mrs. Pitt* still gets turned around."

Thomas nodded knowingly.

"Alanna?" Caleb prodded.

He was no gentleman.

Alanna seethed as she pulled back her shoulders, smiled and marched past Caleb into his room.

She heard the soft click of the lock and felt every muscle in her body tense.

"Best get out of those wet clothes."

"I'm not going to undress in front of you," she whispered, fearing the others would hear.

Caleb moved past her as if he were a cat stalking in its cage. He sat down on his bed and the old springs creaked loudly. He yanked off his socks. "You are going to catch a cold."

Already her skin felt clammy and the cold had settled in her bones. "Once you're finished, I'll change."

"It could be awhile. I was planning on taking a nap."

She hugged her arms around her chest as another shiver passed through her body. "You've never been one to nap. Why start now?"

"I've been up most of the night and spent the last hour and a half fighting the sea. I'm exhausted."

He ran his long fingers through his black hair then reached for the bottom of his sweater. Before she could look away he pulled off the sweater. Like a fool, she all but ogled his finely muscled chest and flat belly. Remembered kissing that belly, following the thin trail of hair that led below his belt buckle.

"You're staring," Caleb said without a hint of emotion. "It's a bad habit you've developed."

Alanna clamped her mouth closed. Heat burned her cheeks and she turned around. A restless energy she'd not felt in a very long time stirred inside her. "I'm not undressing in front of you."

"It's nothing I haven't seen before. Several times as a matter of fact." His deep voice raked over her nerves.

She cringed. "I was unconscious."

"The last time, yes. But not the other times. As I remember you were very much awake."

She closed her eyes. "That's ancient history."

"Sure."

His voice lacked conviction. She wanted to remind him that what they'd shared was gone, but she didn't. The truth was that there was something between them. Like it or not. Good or bad. Something was there, connecting them in ways she could no longer define.

The sooner she was gone from this place the better.

She moistened her lips. "If you would just step out of the room for a moment, I'll change quickly."

She heard his pants hit the floor and his body slide between the sheets and blankets. "This is my room. You don't like the arrangements then leave. Then you can explain who you really are, *Mrs. Pitt.*"

Frustrated, she whirled around and found him lying back on his bed under the covers with his hands tucked behind his head. "If you're determined to be so difficult, why did you help me out in the first place?"

His gaze bore into her and for a moment he did not speak. "Why did you help me today?"

Alanna's frustration melted. "It didn't seem right you going out there alone."

"A lot of women wouldn't have helped. You did help and I appreciate that."

Unexpected fear tightened the muscles in her back. "Is it always so bad when you go out?"

"More often than not."

"Don't you ever worry that you'll drown?"

"Every time."

Pride welled inside her as she thought of him battling the seas. She never could imagine Henry taking such a chance or even her father for that matter. Caleb was a breed apart.

But then she'd known from the beginning that he never fit any mold, or marched to anyone's drummer. He followed his own course. "Thanks for helping me with the Randalls."

"Sure."

She offered a wan smile. "I don't suppose you could dip into this newfound gratitude we're sharing and leave the room for a few minutes."

He unclasped his hands, yawned and nestled

down under the covers. "Sorry, Mrs. Pitt, but either change in here or tell the Randalls the truth."

Alanna gritted her teeth. "You're determined not to make this easy for me."

He rolled on his side as if he were bored. "You could've told the truth."

Caleb yawned again and closed his eyes. Alanna stood there, unsure of what to do. Why did this have to get so complicated?

She'd have stayed dressed as she was if the cold from her wet clothes wasn't seeping into her bones. Shivering, she rubbed her hands over her arms hoping to get warm. She stamped her feet. She paced the room.

"Get out of the damn clothes, Alanna," Caleb said, his eyes still closed.

It struck her then that she was being foolish. Here she was freezing to death because she didn't want him to see her naked. How utterly foolish!

Alanna turned her back to Caleb and reached for the hem of her shirt. She pulled the wet wool over her arms. Cold air met damp skin. Her nipples puckered and she started to shiver. Quickly, she opened the chest and pulled out another sweater. She tugged it over her head and immediately her body started to warm.

She unfastened the buttons on her pants and started to peel the wet fabric over her hips. Her pants were halfway down her legs when Caleb sighed and rolled on his side. Eyes closed, he was facing her.

Keeping her eye on him, she removed the pants and then slipped on a dry set. Caleb's long, lean body took up most of the bed. The sheets and blankets only reached halfway up his torso. Her gaze was drawn to the steady rise and fall of his chest. Even in sleep, his face was tense and tight. He never let his guard down.

As she fastened the top button, she realized Caleb's pants were enormous on her. The sweater reached past her knees and the pants hung a good eight inches past her feet.

Alanna sat down on the trunk and rolled up the pants legs. However, when she stood the waist slipped halfway down her hips.

Fisting a handful of fabric in her hand, she moved to the small mirror on the bureau. Her skin looked a shade paler than normal. Sticking out of her braid were stalks of sea oats. She picked the dry weeds out of her hair, which now felt as coarse as straw. She'd have sold her soul for a comb.

"Top drawer, right side," Caleb said.

Alanna whirled around and found his head propped up on his elbow. "You're awake!"

He rubbed his eye. "You're making enough noise to wake the dead."

"You should have said something."

"Why? Then you'd have stayed in those wet clothes and caught your death." He nodded toward the dresser. "Top drawer on the right."

Caleb stared at her with such intensity that her skin tingled. Her gaze dropped to his muscled chest. She felt her nipples harden.

She blinked. "What?"

"A belt and a comb. You need both."

She gave herself a mental shake. "Yes. A belt. These pants are huge on me."

"One of my better pairs so be careful."

She rummaged through the drawer and found the long black belt. She started to wind it around her waist.

"Why are you doing that? The buckle will dig into your skin."

She hooked the loop through the buckle. The belt was cumbersome but she was warm. "No, it's fine."

"Aren't you coming to bed?"

Nervous laughter bubbled out her. "With you?"

"We've slept together before. Besides, I'm too tired to do anything." He sounded so reasonable, as if he didn't care one way or the other what she did.

She knew better. "Sure you are."

He'd made it clear that he'd sleep with her. He'd also made it clear to her that he didn't love her. She only wished she could say her feelings were as black and white as his. After today, she was beginning to wonder how deeply her feelings for him ran.

He looked all innocence. "Are you afraid of me?"

Alanna was already moving toward the door and reaching for the doorknob when she said over her shoulder, "Like the plague."

Chapter Ten

Alanna didn't care that her muscles ached and that she'd have traded her favorite pair of shoes to sleep in a warm bed. She simply wanted to put distance between her and Caleb.

She wasn't angry with him anymore. She even believed that she had begun to make peace with the past. The problem now was her feelings. They were much like a flowering bulb that had just endured a long cold winter. The sun was out and dormant feelings were coming alive.

She moved into the kitchen. With everyone else asleep, the house was quiet. Toby, who'd been sleeping on his pallet by the stove, thumped his tail. "Hey, boy."

Toby yawned and put his head back down.

Alanna started to clean the dishes the others had left on the table. Stacking the bowls, she placed them next to the sink. She pumped water from the pump by the back door. The water was brackish and discolored, but until the rain stopped and she could get fresh water from the barrels outside, it would have to do.

She scraped the bowls clean, dumping their contents into a garbage bowl. Hearing the spoon click against porcelain, Toby rose and moved slowly over to her. His tail was wagging.

Alanna lifted an eyebrow. "Oh and I suppose you're looking for scraps?"

He barked.

She laughed and kneeling down, set the bowl full of food scraps down. The dog immediately shoved his muzzle in the bowl and started to eat. She stroked his back. He wagged his tail.

"I am going to miss you, boy." She'd also miss the sharp fresh air, the beach and the sound of the crashing waves, which had lulled her to sleep the last couple of nights.

She'd also miss the sense of purpose she'd felt today. She was glad she'd been there for Caleb— to steady him when he'd nearly toppled into the water. She'd been glad she had the skills to cook a hot meal for the Randalls, the boys and Caleb.

Alanna rose and started to dunk the bowls into the cold water.

"I thought you'd be asleep."

Debra Randall's soft voice had Alanna turning. The other woman had changed into an oversize calico dress that Alanna recognized from the large trunk of castoffs. The dress's drooping bodice accentuated Debra's rounded belly. Her face was pale but her eyes bright.

Alanna offered a smile. "I could say the same about you."

Debra, supporting her swollen stomach with her hand, took a seat at the kitchen table. "I know. Thomas is already sleeping heavily. But with the baby's moving, I just couldn't get comfortable."

Fascinated, Alanna asked, "Does he move a lot?"

"A lot. I think he's wearing shoes."

"When is the baby due?"

"November."

Sadness twisted inside Alanna. She thought about the baby she'd carried for only a couple of months. The babe would have been just over a year. It would have been crawling around. Likely it would have had Caleb's black hair and maybe her green eyes.

Alanna's throat tightened. "You must be very excited."

Debra smoothed her hand over her belly as if cradling the babe inside. "We were only just married seven months ago and this baby was a surprise to us. But we are excited.'' She rubbed her hand gently over her belly. ''Thomas wants a boy.''

Caleb would have liked a son. Tears welled in her eyes. Alanna turned back to the sink and tipped her head back so the tears wouldn't spill. ''Have you thought of names?''

The names Debra listed went over Alanna's head. She was too busy, trying to stamp back her own sadness and get control of herself. She pulled in a deep breath. She refused to travel back in time. What mattered was today. ''I like those names,'' Alanna said absently.

Debra wrinkled her nose. ''I'm not so fond of Edgar. But it is Thomas's father's name.''

''Edgar Randall. I like the sound of that.'' She could feel her equilibrium returning. ''So Thomas has a new church in Richmond. You must be very excited.''

Debra nibbled at the bread. ''Thomas is excited.''

Alanna heard the uncertainty in the young woman's voice. She placed the first clean dish on the counter next to the sink. ''And you're not?''

''It's a great opportunity.''

She dunked another dish. ''But...?''

Debra sighed. ''But my family is in Savannah.

I thought we'd be there longer, at least until the baby is born.'' She fingered the cheese. ''And now the ship and all that we owned are lost.''

Alanna had sold so many of her own possessions over the last two years to keep the creditors at bay. She understood the heartache of watching cherished items being carted off one by one. She remembered something Caleb had told her years ago. ''I've heard that when possessions from shipwrecks wash up on shore they're taken to town and auctioned.''

Debra's eyes brightened. ''Do you think some of our things made it?''

Alanna shrugged. ''I can't say, but it's worth asking when the storm clears. I'm sure Caleb will know what to do.'' Caleb seemed to know so much. His confidence—and yes, his arrogance—could be comforting.

She finished washing and stacking the dishes. She dried her hands and then the plates.

Debra took Alanna's hand. ''Thank you again.''

''You've already thanked me twice.''

''I can't thank you enough. When the ship's captain was washed overboard, I was certain we'd die. I was so afraid.''

''Caleb is the real hero. I just helped.''

Debra shook her head. ''I saw the way you held

the boat in place. And when you jumped to your feet and steadied him, it was so brave. He's very lucky to have you at his side today. He couldn't have rescued us without you.''

Alanna doubted that. ''Caleb is so full of fire and vinegar I truly believed he'd have found a way to keep that boat steady while you climbed aboard.''

''You underestimate yourself. You have a brave and compassionate heart, Mrs. Pitt.''

Alanna stiffened. ''Call me Alanna.''

''Alanna,'' the woman said testing the name. ''You don't look like an Alanna.''

Rising, she poured herself a cup of coffee. ''Oh really, why's that?''

''Alannas strike me as spoiled and silly. You're neither of those.''

Alanna laughed as she moved toward the stove. She poured a cup of hot water into a cup and then sprinkled tea leaves into it before she set it in front of Debra. ''Don't be so sure of that. I have very selfish moments.''

Debra warmed her hands around the cup. ''Thank you. I can't imagine you ever being selfish.''

Alanna laughed. She remembered a time when she'd pouted for an entire day because her shoes did not perfectly match the gown she'd ordered for an opening. "Are you hungry? I have more stew."

"Couldn't eat another bite." Debra motioned toward the chair beside her. "Sit and talk with me."

Alanna took the seat. It felt good to get off her feet and she thought again about the warm bed waiting for her. If only Caleb weren't in it.

Debra sipped her tea. "What brought you out here?"

She shrugged. "In truth it was Caleb."

Debra leaned back, nodding as if she understood. "Love is a powerful force. It makes women do many unexpected things."

Love. No, no, no. Her heart began to race at the thought. Yes, she cared for him, but love. No, loving Caleb would be the worst thing that ever happened to her. "I don't know if love is the right word."

Debra's eyes sparkled with interest as she nibbled a piece of cheese. "Then what would you say it was?"

Alanna folded her arms over her chest. "Anger. Frustration. Fury."

"Ah," she chuckled. "My mamma used to say anger and love were the opposite sides of the same coin. I remember when I met my Thomas. He could make me so mad I could spit fire. He liked to tease me. He knew me so well he could push just the right buttons to make me fighting mad. I'll bet it was much like that with you and your Mr. Pitt.''

A faint smile touched her lips. "He used to tease me about the way I wore my hair. He hated it pulled back in a tight chignon—said it made me look like an old-maid schoolteacher. I used to get so mad and he'd just laugh." She'd not thought about that in so long.

Until now each time she visited the past she'd felt nothing but regret. She'd always told herself that she'd been a fool to let Caleb Pitt into her life. As she thought back to that first dinner they'd shared, she remembered the reasons she'd wanted him.

"I'll wager your Mr. Pitt wasn't a patient suitor. He strikes me as a man of action and few words.''

Debra's words struck close to the truth. Caleb had never been one for tender words. "Our first dinner was at my father's house. It was a disaster.''

She leaned closer. "What happened?"

"Father wasn't happy that I'd invited Caleb to dinner. Father thought he was much too rough around the edges and wasn't suitable for me.''

"I'm sure Caleb quickly won your father over."

"Caleb has a habit of speaking exactly what's on his mind. He didn't agree with Father on some discussion about boats and he wasn't afraid to speak his thoughts. Caleb was respectful but he didn't back down. Father wasn't pleased—he was used to always having his way. As I remember, Father asked him to leave early."

"When did you see him again?"

Alanna smiled at the memory. "Two days later. It was at All Saints Church."

Debra clapped her hands in excitement. "Thomas knows the pastor there. Reverend Johnson."

The comment brought her up short and for a moment she couldn't speak. "This story must be boring you."

"Not at all! I want to hear every detail. What happened at the church?"

Alanna became very aware of each word she spoke. She wanted to tell her the truth but feared each word would one day get back to Henry. "We had a clothing drive. Caleb brought a cartload of sweaters and pants—he said it was unclaimed cargo, but I suspect he bought it—the clothes were hardly worn."

Debra pressed her hands to her face. "How sweet."

"It was." She traced circles on the tabletop with her fingertip. "He let it slip that he'd be at a ship auction that afternoon. I went. From there it was dinner almost every night."

Debra's eyes warmed. "When did you know you loved him?"

Alanna let her mind drift. "We were attending a large party. His ship the *Intrepid* was being launched. He'd worked so hard to have that ship built and he was so proud. Everyone wanted to talk to him. He was the man of the day." Absently her hand went to her wrist. "In the midst of it all, he pulled me aside to give me a bracelet. It was so delicate and lovely. He placed it on my wrist and kissed me. I knew then that I loved him." Days later the bracelet had disappeared. She'd torn her room apart looking for it. She'd been too ashamed to tell Caleb of her carelessness.

"Knowing Mr. Pitt now, I'd bet you had a short courtship."

Alanna felt her skin warm. "Caleb had wanted to marry me within two weeks. I'd have married him but Father insisted on a large wedding. I was his only child and he wanted the best for me."

Caleb had been disappointed at the news. He'd

wanted a quiet ceremony in a seaside chapel with just family and very close friends. But she'd tried to convince him that this was something her father wanted to do for them. The extravagant wedding was his way of accepting Caleb. Besides, she'd said, what were a few months when they had a lifetime. In the end, Caleb had agreed to wait.

Now as she thought back she wondered about her father's true intent. Had the wedding plans just been a way to delay their marriage? Had he known then he'd blow up the *Intrepid*?

"Was your wedding a grand affair?" Debra's voice bubbled with excitement.

"Yes," she said absently.

Instead of the lavish dress design, detailed plans and grand guest lists, she remembered the quiet moonlit moment she'd shared with Caleb in his cabin when they'd exchanged vows. In the end it was just the two of them. Perfect.

They'd intended to repeat their vows at the formal wedding, which never was to be. After the accident, she'd spent weeks returning the gifts. She'd written notes of apology until her hands cramped. And then there'd been the baby.

Why did it always come back to the baby? It had been two years since the miscarriage. Tears tightened her throat. "When did this discussion become all about me? My heavens. I am being selfish.''

Debra must have sensed the shift in Alanna's mood. Without a word said, she seemed to know that she had touched on a delicate subject. She patted Alanna on the hand. ''No matter what happened, you're here now and that's all that counts.''

Alanna didn't know what to say. She refused to fabricate another lie when the last one had begun to weigh heavily on her heart.

Abruptly, Debra's eyes widened and her hand slid to her belly. She laughed. ''I think the baby agrees.''

Alanna's eyes widened. ''Is the baby all right?''

She rubbed circles on her belly. ''He just likes to kick me in the ribs every so often so that I don't forget he's there.''

Her baby had never moved. ''What does it feel like?''

Debra took Alanna's hand and laid it on her stomach. ''Let's see if he'll move for you. He can be quite the show-off when it's just the two of us, but when anyone else is close he can be so still. Very maddening for Thomas.''

Alanna sat very still, holding her breath. She'd

known her share of women expecting but she'd never touch their bellies. It simply wasn't done.

"Your stomach is rock-hard. Is that normal?" Alanna asked.

"My mother says yes."

Debra's stomach rose and fell with each breath she took, but there was no sign of the baby.

"Maybe he's asleep?" Alanna whispered.

"He's awake. He's just being difficult. Give him another minute."

As the seconds clicked by, Alanna's disappointment grew. She wanted so much to feel the baby move. Then just as she was about to withdraw her hand, she felt a fluttering under her hands. "Oh my!"

Debra nodded, satisfied. "Meet Edgar Thomas Davis Randall."

Tears burned her eyes. "Like butterfly wings."

Debra groaned. "More like a butterfly with an anvil or hammer."

On cue, the baby kicked hard under Alanna's hand. She drew back her hand, laughing. "Oh my! That must be so wonderful."

Debra's eyes softened. "It is. I can't wait to hold him in my arms."

Alanna imagined her own baby in her arms. And abruptly the joy of the moment evaporated. Again, she was faced with all that she'd lost.

Lost. No, lost was not the right word. She'd not lost Caleb. She had tossed him aside. If she'd not been so impulsive or if she had had the courage to face up to her father after the accident, she could have had a life with him. There was no saving the first child but there could have been another baby.

Debra studied Alanna. "Are you all right?"

"Yes." No.

"You and Mr. Pitt will have children one day," she said softly.

Sadness jolted Alanna. There'd be no other children for her and Caleb and the realization tore at her heart. She wanted to explain everything to Debra, but she denied the impulse. No good would come of it. "You are very kind."

Again, Debra seemed to understand the power of the emotions in Alanna. She made a point of yawning widely. "I think the day's turmoil is finally catching up with me. Perhaps, I had best retire. Are you going to be all right alone?"

"I'm fine. And you should rest."

Debra rose. "I shall sleep like the dead."

Alanna smiled. "If you need anything just knock on my door."

Cupping her hand under her rounded belly, Debra rose. "Second door on the right?"

Alanna opened her mouth to correct Debra, and

then she caught herself. Caleb's room was the second on the right. The young sailors now slept in her room. "Yes."

Debra hugged Alanna. "Thank you again, Mrs. Pitt. Alanna."

Taken aback for a moment, Alanna stood stiff. Then slowly she raised her arms and hugged Debra back. A sense of happiness spread through her. "I'm glad we were here for you."

Debra drew back. She looked tired. However, this time the woman wasn't trying to smooth over a delicate moment. She was truly exhausted.

"Go to bed," Alanna ordered.

"Yes, ma'am."

Alanna watched as the young woman lumbered down the long hallway to her room. When she closed the door behind her, Alanna turned back to the kitchen. Since she'd arrived this room had felt like a haven. Here she felt safe.

But as soon as she'd wiped off the tabletop and filled Toby's water bowl, the weariness overtook her. Suddenly, she could barely keep her eyes open.

All the rooms were full and if she wanted to sleep in a bed, it would have to be Caleb's. There was the couch in the parlor, but if Debra or any of the others came looking for her in the middle of the night it would make for an awkward situation.

Alanna moved down the hallway to Caleb's door. She pressed her hand against the cold wood as if somehow she could gauge whether or not he was sleeping. Her heartbeat thrummed in her fingertips as she waited.

Encouraged by the silence, she wrapped her fingers around the cold knob and slowly opened the door. She peeked inside. The room was dark, and she could hear Caleb's deep even breathing.

He had to be exhausted. A part of her softened as she pictured him again, battling the seas.

Nibbling her lip, she eased into the room and closed the door behind her. It clicked and she flinched, half expecting him to wake. She waited for fear the slight sound would wake him. He'd always been such a light sleeper.

Stay asleep, please! Desperately she wanted to slip into the bed without him knowing.

When she didn't hear him stir, she tiptoed across the floor. Closer, she could see he lay on his side, his face to the wall.

The bed was large enough for the two of them and all she needed was a couple of hours of sleep. Alanna lifted the covers.

Caleb shoved out a breath.

Alanna stopped breathing. When he didn't

move, she released a silent breath. With her clothes on, she slipped under the blankets, careful not to jostle the mattress. She stayed so close to the edge of the bed, her right foot peeked out from under the covers.

Despite the awkward position, the warmth of the blankets slowly started to seep into her bones. After several minutes, Caleb remained asleep. She started to relax.

This was going to work. She could get a few hours of sleep and be gone before Caleb was the wiser.

Caleb awoke. Instantly, he was aware of Alanna beside him in bed. And he was stiff as a poker.

Chapter Eleven

In a perfect world, Caleb would be driving into Alanna right this very moment. She'd be wrapping her naked legs around him as she accepted all of him. He'd hear her soft moans in his ear and feel her fingers clinging to his back. He'd kiss her breasts, coaxing the nipples into soft peaks and listening to her cries of pleasures as he found his release.

Lord knows, he'd dreamed of stripping her down naked and making love to her enough times over the last two years.

But this world was far from perfect.

With sheer will, Caleb reined in his desires. He clamped down on the need driving him and tried to ignore the way his body throbbed with unspent desire.

Alanna moaned and wriggled her bottom against him.

It was going to be a long night.

Muttering an oath, he rolled on his back and tucked his hands behind his head. He stared at the bands of moonlight that slashed across the ceiling. He counted to ten. He thought about the storm's damage and the days of work it would take to repair everything. He imagined cold rain pelting his body.

Yet, the harder he tried to ignore Alanna, the more her sweet scent floated around him. From the corner of his eye, he noted the way her rosy lips parted slightly as she slept. His gaze skimmed down the length of her delicate jaw to the curve of her neck to the gentle rise and fall of her chest.

He rolled on his side and faced her. As he stared at the thick cable sweater, he remembered how the sea had ruined her undergarments. He knew she wore no corset or chemise. If he were to slip his hand under the sweater his fingertips would touch the warm flesh of her flat belly. Inches away, he'd find the naked underside of her breast. Even after two years he remembered how her breast fit so well in the palm of his hand.

Caleb's erection began to ache. He groaned.

God, what was he doing to himself?

Entertaining these thoughts was folly at best. He had plenty of things that were far more important to think about other than Alanna. And still, his thoughts circled back to her.

Aye, she'd been brave today. Hell, she'd been more than brave. She'd been a warrior goddess who had held on to the oars when he knew she was terrified. And when he'd lost his balance and nearly fallen into the sea, her cool hands wrapped around his waist and steadied him.

He was in her debt.

Sighing, he sat up and swung his legs over the side of the bed. A bit of bravery did not change all the barriers that stood between them.

Caleb raked his hands through his hair. He refocused on the chores that needed doing. The surfboat would need to be dried and restocked. The lenses in the lighthouse would need polishing. There'd be rope that needed rewinding. He'd work until he'd worn out his body, until he could barely keep his eyes open. By then, pray God, the storm would have passed and everyone would leave him alone on the island.

Alone. He thought about the years ahead—the years that would be spent alone.

He glanced back over his shoulder at Alanna. Even in sleep, the worry lines remained on her forehead and around the corners of her mouth.

The sprinkling of freckles across the bridge of her nose caught his attention. He swore he'd remember every detail of her face, but he didn't remember the freckles. But then he'd never seen her face washed clean. Alanna had been a vain woman and she'd liked her powders and lotions. There'd been a time when he'd taken great pride in her appearance. She was a woman any man would like to have on his arm.

But seeing her faced scrubbed clean, he was struck by how young she was. Her birthday had been just over a month ago and he knew she'd turned twenty-one. Had she been only eighteen when he'd met her? She'd moved with the grace and poise of an older woman so it had been easy for him to forget she was so young.

He liked her better like this. Clean and natural, he felt as if he was seeing the true woman this time.

Gently, he brushed a curl from her forehead.

Every day these last two years, especially during the darkest days after the accident, he'd thought about her. At first, he longed for her and then after she'd refused him, he'd cursed her.

But no matter how angry or lonely he was, he conjured the image of her long blond hair, the gentle curve of her nose, and the faint cleft in her chin. Try as he might, he simply could not let go of her.

Aye, no matter what had happened in the past

or what would happen tomorrow, she'd been amazing today. Most women would have weighed the risks, then run screaming from such a dangerous rescue.

Not Alanna.

She was as impulsive and fearless as ever. A half smile tipped the edge of his lips.

Alanna stirred, then rolled on her side toward him. She started to mumble as if she were trying to say something. A tear streamed down her face and then abruptly she started awake. Gripping her belly, she stared wide-eyed at the ceiling as if she was unsure of where she was. Her breathing quickened and she sat up.

He touched her shoulder. "You're safe."

She started and pulled away.

"Easy," he said.

Slowly her wild gaze focused and she realized where she was. She swung her legs over the side of the bed and pressed the heel of her hand into her forehead. "How long have I been asleep?"

"Not long."

She nodded. "It feels like it's been days."

He swung his body back on the bed and moved behind her. "You're exhausted and I doubt fully recovered from your fever."

"I'm fine." She cleared her throat. "I should check on Debra. She may be hungry."

"The house is quiet. No one else is up. Lie back down."

She shook her head. "I don't think that's too wise."

"Alanna, we're both too tired to do much of anything." He tried to keep his voice even, disinterested. "You need the sleep."

She pushed her bangs off her face. "I'm fine." Rising, she padded over to the hearth and spread her fingertips out to the glowing embers. "Debra is worried about her possessions. They carried everything they owned with them on the boat."

Her voice sounded far away, distant. "I'm sorry to hear that."

She tossed a small log on the fire. The embers spit and popped, then started to lick the edges of the log. "When the ship breaks apart, will the goods wash up on the beach?"

He rolled on his side and propped his head on his palm. The strain on her face puzzled him. "Sometimes."

"Is there a way to track down their things if they do?"

"It would be tough. But not impossible. Why the sudden concern? You barely know the Randalls."

She poked at the embers with a stick. "I like

Debra. She's got a good heart.'' She shoved out a sigh. "And she's expecting a baby."

"Aye."

Firelight glowed on her profile. "It's their first. Due in November."

The hint of sadness in her voice tugged at him. "Why do you care so much?"

She shrugged. "It's got to be scary. She's lost just about everything and she's got a baby on the way."

Instinct had Caleb rising. He couldn't say what it was about her, but he knew something was wrong. He tugged on his pants and moved to the fire and squatted next to her. "Alanna? There's more to this than the Randall's furniture."

She sighed, and then tossed the stick onto the flames. "There isn't really."

"Like it or not, I do know your moods. I know when something is wrong." For a long time she stared at the flames. He'd begun to think she'd not tell him what was wrong.

She brushed a tear from her cheeks. "After the accident, our friends abandoned me. And Father was so distraught over his business he had little time."

Her quiet even voice held his attention. He understood she wasn't complaining. She was simply setting the stage for something else. Something bigger. So he waited for her to continue.

"In one moment I seemed to have the world in my hands and the next I'd lost everything. The creditors started arriving almost immediately after the accident. And for a time I thought we'd lose the house."

He'd heard about Obadiah's financial troubles and at the time he'd been glad. He'd wanted the old man to suffer. He'd wanted Alanna to suffer. Yet, as he looked at her right now, she looked so very small, so vulnerable. And he regretted all the hell he'd wished upon her.

Alanna was silent for so long that he thought she wouldn't speak and then she said, "I found out I was pregnant."

He could feel the blood drain from his head. His world started to spin. A baby! Was the child a boy or girl? What was his name? So many questions, so many possibilities. "Good God, Alanna!"

Another tear trickled down her cheek and she savagely whipped it away. "I lost our baby eight weeks into the pregnancy."

For only moments the possibility of a child existed in his mind, yet he'd bounced from shock to joy to sadness. Caleb felt a crushing sense of loss.

While he'd been in the hospital going through his own private hell, Alanna had been trapped in hers.

Suddenly, he wanted to take her in his arms and grieve for the child they'd both lost. He laid his hand on her shoulder. The weight of all they'd lost suddenly was more than he could bear. "I wish I'd been there for you."

She laid her hand over his. For the first time in years, he felt the deep connection he'd once shared with her. It warmed his body, melting the ice in his veins. His heart beat faster, as if it had been in limbo and now had come back to life. The hate and anger vanished with the ice and a weight lifted from his shoulders.

"I should have had the courage to be there for you, but I was so afraid. Father would have thrown me into the streets if he'd known I was pregnant and there wasn't a friend that would have taken me in." She closed her eyes. "God help me, but I didn't want to be poor or alone. And the thought of caring for a child alone terrified me."

He tried to clear his mind of emotion and think. "What happened?"

She pulled her hand away and stared into the flames. "The night before your trial started, I began cramping. I lost the baby two days later."

He remembered the day of the trial and how

he'd cursed her for not coming to him. "I came to your house the night after the inquest."

She swallowed back tears. "Father never told me you came, but if he had I couldn't have seen you. I was too ill with terrible bleeding. I refused to tell anyone what was going on. One of my maids panicked when she saw the blood and sent for the doctor. He helped me and I begged him to keep my secret. He did."

"No one knows."

"No one."

"I would have moved heaven and earth to be with you, if I'd known."

A faint smile touched her lips. "I know."

He reached out for her, but this time she drew away. The brief connection they'd shared was breaking and there wasn't anything he could do about it. Fisting his fingers at his side he fought the urge to speak.

"That's why I didn't respond to your letters. It was all just too painful."

He remembered the angry words in his second letter. All his frustration had spilled onto the page. He was glad now she'd not read them. "The letters are best forgotten."

"I'd always taken money and security for granted until that time. I'd never once worried where I'd live or feared if there would be enough food. But as the world around me started to crumble, I began to worry." She sniffed. "You would not recognize Father's house now. I've sold everything inside it to pay the creditors. My mother's jewels, the silver. Everything is gone save for a few pieces of furniture. The house sold at auction two months ago. I've been staying with Henry's aunt since then."

He would spend the rest of his days protecting her. Her world would never shatter again. "Those days are past, Alanna. You are safe now."

She shook her head. "Safe is an illusion without money. I know that now."

"Debra Randall isn't afraid."

"She's a brave woman."

"You faced that surf today. You are brave."

"Not like Debra. Her bravery is the quiet strong kind that lasts a lifetime. Mine is always short-lived. It's not consistent."

She was wrong.

He laid his hands on her shoulders and turned her toward him. Time had changed her from a girl into a woman. At first he'd not seen it, but now he did. The spark remained in her eyes, the same fearlessness pulsed in her veins, but there was also wisdom. "You are a different woman now, Alanna. You can weather any storm, I'll wager."

As if he hadn't spoken she shook her head and

moved to the window and stared through the clouded panes of glass. Outside the wind howled and the rain pelted the earth with uncommon ferocity. "Strength does not pay creditors, Caleb. Nor does it keep a child fed and warm. The only reason I didn't lose the house two years ago was because of Henry."

"Henry." He wished a curse on the man.

"I know you don't like Henry. But he was a good friend to me when no one else was. And he's offering me security."

"The finest house in the world is a cold, sterile place without love."

She pressed her fingertips against the glass. "Henry loves me."

He could see her face reflected in the glass. "Henry's love is an illusion."

She shook her head. "Our love was an illusion, Caleb. When we were tested, we failed."

He closed the distance between them. "We didn't make it through the first gale, that I'll grant you. But given a second chance, we might make it through just fine."

"There's no hope for us."

His fingers on her shoulders tightened. "Then why are you here?"

"At first it was to deliver the box. And then I thought it was to answer the questions surrounding Father's suicide. But now I see that I was meant to come here. To see that you were well and to tell you about the baby. I had to come here to close the chapter on our life together. Now I see that I am better suited as Henry's wife. When I return home, I am going to accept his marriage proposal.''

Savage hot jealousy constricted his chest as he listened to her talk of marrying another man. He hated the idea of another man looking at her, let alone making love to her. The idea of her lying naked under Henry, her glorious curls strewn on the pillow, gnawed at his gut.

He remembered how it had been with them. Her passion had been unbridled. She'd savored his kisses and matched his desire with one just as fevered. The nights they'd shared had held the promise of a lifetime of passion. He knew time would only make them better lovers as they discovered each other's bodies and learned how to stoke the flames in the other.

Now, Henry would be learning the curves of her body. Henry would kiss the tender flesh at the base of her neck.

If he had a whit of sense, he'd send her away with that damn box of hers. But like a dam bursting, two years of desire exploded free. He pulled her to him and drew her to his chest. She stared wide-eyed up at him, her hand pressed to his chest. He could feel her warm breath on his face and the rapid beating of her pulse in her wrist.

He covered her lips with a hard and possessive kiss. His hand slipped under her sweater to the naked flesh of her back. He pressed the small of her back into his hard arousal.

Her scent mingled with her taste, inflaming his senses. Like a man lost in the desert, he greedily drank her in. He wanted to strip the clothes from her body and lay her on the bed. He imagined her wild and naked as she'd been years before, begging for his touch, calling his name in her husky, fevered voice.

She rose on tiptoe and wrapped her arms around his neck. Her desire was an aphrodisiac, inflaming him in ways he'd never dreamed possible.

He drove his tongue between her lips, determined to give her so much pleasure that all the miseries of the past were forgotten.

A soft moan rumbled in her chest and she relaxed against him, giving herself to the kiss. This was the Alanna he remembered, the woman who'd haunted his dreams.

When he broke the kiss, he stared down at her wide-eyed expression, a mixture of passion and horror.

His breathing was ragged, as if he'd just run the length of the beach. "It's better than I remembered."

"I'd hoped it wouldn't be," she whispered. "I wanted to hate touching you."

He reached out to her. "But you don't."

Shaking her head, she stepped back from him. "No."

"This isn't what I expected or bargained for, Alanna, but it feels right."

"Feelings get me into trouble. When I rely on feelings, I end up making terrible mistakes."

His mind clearing, he saw the fear in her eyes. "This isn't a mistake."

She pressed her fingertips to her lips. "It is. We don't fit anymore. We belong in different worlds." Lifting her chin, she moved away from him toward the door. "It's truly over between us."

Quietly, she left.

As he stood alone in his room, her scent still clung to him. His fingertips still tingled from touching her.

"It's not over between us, Alanna. Not by a long shot."

Chapter Twelve

Alanna's head was spinning as she made her way down the hallway toward the back door. At this point she didn't care if it was raining or not. She needed to get outside.

She sat on the bench by the back door and pulled on her boots, still damp and cold from the rescue.

Trembling hands made lacing up the first boot a struggle. Toby came up to her, his tail wagging. He barked and nudged her hands. "I know, boy, this place is getting a little small for me, too."

Hadn't the last two years taught her anything? She'd been trapped in a living nightmare since she'd foolishly given her heart to Caleb. She'd paid a high price for her passionate nature. Yet, here she was nearly surrendering herself to him again.

Fool me once, shame on you.

Fool me twice, shame on me.

The taste of him lingered on her lips. She was no longer a silly girl just out of the schoolroom with too much bravado and not enough sense. She understood how destructive passion could be and she'd not make that mistake again.

It was more imperative than ever that she marry Henry. He was calm, even and he would never make her blood sing with his kisses. Together, they would build a good, stable life together.

Flexing her stiff fingers, she tied the laces in a bow on the first boot. It was more important now that the Randalls not know who she really was. The trick now was keeping a safe distance from *her husband.*

Sighing, she yanked on the second boot.

"You ain't going out in that mess are you?"

The sound of the young man's voice had Alanna lifting her head. There stood Alex and Ryan. Each wore Caleb's castoffs.

The tall, gangly boy, Ryan, was a bit too tall for the pants and sweater he wore. His sleeves and pants legs were a couple of inches too short whereas his friend had to roll up his pants and sweater. Alex, who was shorter and stockier, had rolled up his pants and shirtsleeves. Neither possessed Caleb's muscular build and both looked as if they'd stepped out of the schoolroom.

Alanna forced her muscles to relax and smiled at the boys. "I just need a bit of fresh air."

Alex and Ryan exchanged glances. By their expressions it was clear they thought she'd gone daft.

"The wind will sweep you away," Ryan said.

"I should be just fine." She kept her voice light as if walking in a gale was normal.

Alex shook his head. "Ma'am, the trees is bent sideways in the wind."

"Sideways?" Alanna hesitated. She rose and looked out the back window. Wind and rain swept across the yard. She groaned. Lord, but she wanted out of this place, but the last thing she needed was to stumble into trouble, and then have Caleb come and rescue her again.

"Perhaps you're right." Like it or not, she was stuck.

She started back toward the kitchen. The cottage seemed to shrink by the moment. Out of politeness, she said, "Can I fix you anything to eat?"

The boys nodded. "Thanks, ma'am," Ryan said.

The boys were bottomless pits, she decided. "You really are hungry?"

"We're still hungry enough to eat a whale," Alex said.

Just hours ago, they'd eaten more in one sitting than she did in a week. "Well, then, have a seat."

Still, within ten minutes she'd reheated the stew and sliced each thick pieces of bread. Her nerves had calmed and she felt her control return.

Ryan ate his food as if he were half-starved. "We sure do appreciate your helping Caleb yesterday. I was sure we was gonna go down with the boat."

Alanna sat at the table across from them. Puppies. They were like growing puppies, she thought. "I'm glad we could help."

Alex swallowed a mouthful of cheese. "When we hit that shoal, my first thought was of Captain Pitt. I knew he'd be keeping watch."

"So you know Mr. Pitt?"

Ryan nodded. "Ain't many in these parts that don't know the captain."

Alanna watched Alex gobble another piece of sausage.

She wondered if the boy had a hollow leg. "I suppose they've gotten to know him these last couple of years."

"That and from before," Alex said.

"Before?"

"My uncle Sloan served with the captain in the Navy."

"Sloan? Does he own the tavern in town?"

Ryan's face brightened. "Yep. He's the one."

Alex mopped up his stew with a piece of bread. "Uncle Sloan didn't say anything about the captain marrying," Ryan said.

She kept her voice even. "It was very recent."

"Wait until Ma hears this news," Alex said.

Slipping out of Easton unnoticed grew more difficult each day. "Your mother knows the captain too?"

"They're first or second cousins," Alex said.

"Cousins?" Caleb had family here? "I read in one of the old journals about another lightkeeper named Pitt."

"That was Caleb's pa," Ryan said.

Caleb was from Easton? She tried to hide her surprise. *November 1866, Keeper Pitt died today.* Caleb would have been about ten. So much made sense now. He'd come to these shores because to him they were home. "Caleb hasn't told me much about his time in Easton."

"The Pitts have been working the lighthouses for fifty years," Alex said. "They've saved hundreds and hundreds of lives. But I guess the captain's told you that."

"Actually, no. He doesn't talk much about himself."

In all the time they'd shared he'd never told her about Easton or the lighthouses. Why hadn't he told her about himself?

"Caleb's father was a famous keeper," Ryan added. "He took care of this very lighthouse right up until the day he died. His pa drowned saving eighteen fishermen who'd gotten caught in a gale.

Alanna's heart tightened. "What happened to his mother?"

"According to my aunt," Alex said, "Captain Pitt's ma wasn't from this area. She didn't like it much here. The wind and the long days alone ate away at her."

"Why didn't she leave after her husband died?"

"Didn't have the money," Ryan said. "She lived in Easton. She was a seamstress and took in laundry. As time went by, she grew to hate the town. My aunt says she turned the captain against this place."

Alex rose and refilled his bowl with stew. "Once the captain's mother died, he wanted no part of this place."

So Caleb had joined the Navy and later moved to Richmond, where he'd played the part of the rising young shipping executive, made friends and enjoyed tremendous success for a time.

Now that she thought back, she could see Caleb had never seemed truly happy when he wasn't on his ship or near the docks. There'd been a stiffness in his shoulders and she'd always sensed he was on guard.

Here he moved with confidence and ease, whether he was dragging a boat into the surf or striding across the lawn fighting a gale.

The truth was, Caleb was as much a part of Lighthouse Island as the wind and surf.

He belonged here.

An hour later, Alanna wasn't sure what caused the fight between Alex and Ryan. She'd been pulling biscuits from the oven when she'd heard them in the parlor, shouting.

Her only thought was to quiet them down. Debra and Thomas needed their sleep.

With a wooden spoon in her hand she hurried into the parlor ready to give each a piece of her mind. She found Alex holding Ryan around his neck as if he were wrestling a shark.

Ryan swung at Alex's midsection. "Let go of me, you underside of a barnacle."

Alex absorbed the punch and tightened his hold

around Ryan's neck. "Not until you give me back that letter and say you is sorry."

"You want it, get it yourself," Ryan shouted.

Alex muttered an oath. "Give it to me."

"Lower your voices." Without thinking Alanna moved between the two just as Ryan pulled his fist back a second time.

Alanna never saw the punch coming.

The next thing she knew she felt a crack of pain and her head snapped back. She stumbled backward a couple of steps, aware that the boys wore horrified expressions. Then she fell to her knees.

She was only vaguely aware of strong arms catching her and of being held close before she passed out.

When Alanna woke she knew she was cradled in Caleb's arms. "What happened?" she muttered.

"Shh," he whispered. "Stay still until I can get you into a bed."

She didn't fight the embrace but relaxed against him. Her head ached and she couldn't seem to raise her head. She winced as her head touched the soft pillows.

"Is she all right?" Alex said.

"You best stay back, boy." Caleb's voice was tense with rage.

"I didn't mean to hit her," Ryan said. "I was aiming for Alex. I didn't even see her."

"Yeah," Alex added. "He was just winding back when she came up. He didn't mean to hit her."

Ryan sounded helpless. "It happened so fast, I couldn't stop."

Alanna winced when Caleb brushed her hair away from her bruised jaw. "They were fighting," she whispered. Lord, but it hurt to talk. "I wanted to stop them. Debra needs her rest."

"She's awake now." Caleb swore under his breath. "Hell, when are you two boys going to learn to stay out of trouble? I told you a month ago not to sail on the *Annabelle Lee* because Captain Jamison was a fool."

Ryan nudged Alex. "I told you he wasn't going to be happy about that."

Alex shrugged. "He was paying well."

Caleb snorted. "Well he's likely at the bottom of the ocean now. So you won't be collecting a nickel."

Alanna opened her eyes. The vision was blurred at first but slowly it began to clear. She could just make out the worry lines etched in Caleb's face. "Don't be mad at the boys. I'm fine. It was my own fault."

Thomas and Debra hurried into the room.

Thomas carried a basin and Debra a towel. Thomas set the basin down on the bedside table.

Debra handed a cloth to Caleb. "Is she all right?"

"Aye, but she'll have a bruise on her cheek."

Ryan leaned forward. "She still got all her teeth?"

Caleb winced as if the idea was too troubling to entertain.

"Nothing worse than getting a tooth knocked out," Alex said. "Last summer in Richmond when I was working the docks a sailor didn't like the look of me. He punched me square in the face. Knocked my molar clean out. Blood everywhere."

"Thanks, Alex," Caleb said. "We can do without the details right now."

Alanna looked up into Caleb's eyes. The way her head felt, she wouldn't be surprised if a few were missing. "How does it look?" she said showing her teeth.

"They're all there."

"Are you sure?"

His gaze was sure and steady. "I wouldn't lie to you."

Relief mingled with guilt. He'd never lied to her. She'd just never had the strength to believe in him. "Thanks." She closed her eyes.

Caleb dunked the rag in the basin and wrung it out. Gently, he pressed the cloth to Alanna's face. "It'll help with the swelling."

She grimaced.

He cursed as if seeing her in pain was more than he could tolerate. "For two smart boys, you two act like you don't have a lick of sense between you. What were you fighting about anyway?"

The boys fell silent.

Opening her eyes, Alanna worked her jaw back and forth. It wasn't broken but she guessed it would be sore for days. "I heard something about a letter?"

The corner of Ryan's mouth tipped into a grin. "A letter from *Jennifer*."

Alex faced Ryan. "I swear if you say her name again, I'll knock you flat."

"Enough!" Caleb shouted.

Alanna touched Caleb's hand. "It's all right. They didn't mean any harm. Fighting over girls at that age is part of growing up."

Alex grinned at Caleb. "You're one to talk. You snuck up to Virginia last month and got yourself a wife without telling anyone."

Caleb glowered at Alex. The boy drew back.

Ryan kept his distance. "Ain't there ever been a woman you was willing to fight for?"

A wave of sadness washed through Alanna as she saw the tension tighten Caleb's shoulders. How long had he fought for her before he gave up?

"There's no harm done," she whispered.

Ryan moved closer to her bed, careful to give Caleb a wide berth. "We is real sorry, Mrs. Pitt. I didn't mean to hit you. Honest."

She smiled, and then winced. "Don't give it another thought." She eased herself up into a sitting position.

Caleb reached for the pillow and fluffed it behind her head. "Easy."

"Alex, is she pretty?" Alanna asked.

Alex hooked his thumbs in his front pockets. "Jennifer. Yes, ma'am, she's real pretty."

"Does she know you like her?" Alanna said. She moved her jaw from side to side, working the stiffness from it.

Alex frowned. "No! And I don't want her knowing that!"

"Why not?"

"Because. Then everything between us is going to change."

Alanna lifted an eyebrow. "Why is that so bad?"

"If we was to start courting, she'd learn right quick that I don't have much more than a nickel to my name. Seth Davis gave his girl a bright blue ribbon. I ain't got the money for stuff like that.''

Caleb expelled a breath. ''That's why you signed on the *Annabelle Lee*.''

''Yes, sir.''

''If she likes you she won't care about silly presents,'' Debra said. ''Thomas and I have lost everything, but our love is strong.''

Alanna nodded. ''It's not about presents. She just needs to know you will be there and that you will care for her always.''

Caleb rose and walked to the window.

The boy groaned. ''You make it all sound so simple.''

''It is.'' Her heart went out to Alex. She swung her legs over the side.

Debra nudged the two boys. ''Let's get out of here. Mrs. Pitt needs a moment to collect herself.''

Caleb waited for the bedroom door to close before he spoke. ''Did you mean what you just said?'' Caleb said.

Alanna's head throbbed. ''Of course, I meant it.''

His face tightened and then he strode out of the room.

As the sun rose, Caleb stood on the lighthouse crow's nest staring out at the ocean. The rain and wind had stopped, and the air smelled clean and fresh. Soon the sun would heat the earth and breathe life back into the land.

To his surprise, the ship had endured the worst of the storm. She listed badly and would likely break up before week's end but for now she was intact.

Soon a boat would come from the mainland to check on him and to see if there was news of the *Annabelle Lee,* which by now would have been reported overdue.

His life would return to what it had been. Quiet. Peaceful. Desolate.

Gripping the railing, he watched the sun rise and drip bits of light on the dark waters.

He no longer wanted to spend his days out here, alone, waiting for another storm and another wreck. Two years he'd lived in a purgatory of his own making and now he wanted it to end.

He wanted Alanna.

On the ashes of their past life, he wanted to rebuild. Together they could have a fine life here.

He'd seen more life in her these last few days than he had in the months they'd spent together in Richmond. This place had the power to breathe life, to heal and he knew she belonged here.

Of course, she didn't know that.

She still believed her place was with Henry in a world of parties and endless social engagements—a world that would one day squeeze the life from her. She still believed Henry could make her happy.

Now it was his job to prove her wrong. To show her that this was her home; that he was her future.

The question now was how. In the past when he'd set out to woo her, he'd given her a gold bracelet. He remembered taking a good hour at the jeweler's choosing the gold link bracelet, which had cost him more than he earned in a month now. But cost hadn't mattered to him then.

He'd had the jeweler wrap the bracelet in simple white paper. The bow had been red. He'd been so proud of himself. This was the finest gift he'd ever given any woman.

Alanna's eyes had sparkled when she opened the package and when she'd seen the bracelet she'd smiled and thanked him. He placed it around her wrist and kissed her.

But two days later she'd stopped wearing the bracelet. When he'd asked her about it, she promised to wear it again. But she hadn't. It wasn't that she hadn't appreciated the gift, but he'd come to realize that the piece was just one of the many trinkets she possessed.

Caleb stared at the torn sails of the *Annabelle Lee*. What a waste. She was a fine vessel and it sickened him to see her end so tragically.

As he turned from the ocean, he stopped and swung his gaze back to the schooner. A smiled curved the edges of his mouth.

He had found his gift to Alanna.

Chapter Thirteen

Saving the Randalls' goods was the perfect gift for Alanna. It would touch her heart better than any bauble or bit of silk.

Caleb found the boys and Thomas on the beach and told them of his plan to salvage the goods. Thomas had been thrilled and the boys had been more than happy to make up for the morning's mishap.

Feeling proud of himself, he strode across the lawn and into the house. He moved down the hallway and found the women in the parlor. A fire crackled in the hearth. Alanna and Debra had pulled two upholstered chairs near the fire and set a small table between them. They were playing cards.

"Mrs. Randall," Caleb said striding into the room. "I think I might be able to help you with your possessions."

Alanna's green gaze met his. They sparkled with hope and apprehension. He couldn't have asked for a greater gift. ''Do you know these scavengers in town? Can you bargain with them?''

''Better than that,'' he said moving into the room. ''The *Annabelle Lee* is still out on the sandbar where we left her last night. She's listing badly but she has not sunk. By the looks of her, she might hold for a few more days before she goes down. I think if the lads, Thomas and I row out there this morning we might be able to retrieve some of your belongings.''

Debra beamed. ''Are you sure? It was so dangerous out there yesterday.''

''The water's smooth as glass,'' Caleb said.

Alanna frowned. ''Are you sure that it's safe?''

Her concern pleased him. ''With no wind and rain to fight, it'll be easy for us.''

Alanna rose, her hands clasped in excitement. ''Oh, Caleb, that is a wonderful idea! But is it legal for you to go on the ship?''

If he'd given her diamonds or gold he could not have asked for a better reaction. ''Once a ship is scuttled like the *Annabelle Lee,* she's fair game for anyone.''

Debra beamed. ''God bless you, Captain Pitt.''

But it was only Alanna he saw. She stared at

him with such happiness in her eyes. He felt tender warmth spread through his body. At this moment, he'd have done anything for her.

Caleb cleared his throat. "Mrs. Randall, I need for you to make a list of the items you need recovered. The boys have mapped out the ship.

"We are going to have to move quickly. The beach will be crawling with other scavengers soon enough."

Alanna felt more alive than she had in years.

The gentle ocean breeze flapped the folds of her coat as she stood on the beach. Her palm to her forehead, she shaded her hand over her eyes and stared at the wreck of the *Annabelle Lee*. The ship's mast was broken and her large white sails floated on the water. Though she listed badly toward shore, her hull was intact.

The sea was smooth, and the gulls had emerged from their nests and now circled above. Oddly, the wreck was little more than a hundred feet from shore. Last night, surrounded by the darkness and cold, the ship had seemed a million miles away.

Caleb and the other men had been working on the boat for over an hour, when as Caleb predicted the other scavengers had started to arrive. They came in rowboats, sailboats and fishing boats. Old and young men, women and children piloted the boats. A dozen in all, their boats dotted the waters around the *Annabelle Lee* like sharks waiting for the kill. All were eager to board the doomed vessel, but in deference to Caleb they waited.

Alanna watched as Caleb lowered a large chest tied to a rope to the surfboat. His thighs braced apart, his broad well-muscled shoulders bunched under his sweater as he eased the rope through his gloved hands.

She'd never felt such pride as she watched him. In the past she'd seen his confidence and arrogance as a weakness. Now, she realized both were essential if a man challenged the sea.

Already the Randalls' belongings were strewn on the beach as they dried in the fading sun.

The surfboat laden with the last of the Randalls' items rode a wave into shore. As it skimmed the sand Caleb and the other men hopped out into the ankle-deep water. Together, they pulled the boat far enough up the shore so that the waves could not pull it back to the ocean. Caleb and Thomas unloaded a large chest while the boys carried a wooden crate.

Excitement bubbled in Alanna as she watched Debra inspecting her belongings.

Caleb and Thomas set the chest on the beach. All the men's breathing was labored, but it was Caleb who recovered first.

Caleb was drenched. The heavy cotton clung to his chest and narrow waist, and Alanna felt a familiar stirring inside of her. Again she wanted what she'd long ago given up rights to. Her heart tightened. She tried not to let her own sense of loss overshadow her friend's happiness.

Debra ran up to Thomas, who labored up the beach. "This is wonderful!" She kissed her husband full on the lips, uncaring who was around.

Alanna lifted her gaze to Caleb. They'd kissed like that once. As if he read her thoughts, he stared back at her. Heat radiated through her limbs. Her mouth felt suddenly dry.

Unable to bear his scrutiny, she shifted her gaze to the water. Already the other boats had moored alongside the *Annabelle Lee* and people had boarded her and were carting off salvage. Thomas brushed the wet hair from his face and smiled. "I think we got most of it."

Debra wrapped her arm around Thomas and together they walked down the beach.

Caleb approached Alanna. "I envy them."

Hugging her arms around her chest, she faced him. His dark gaze pinned her and she found it difficult to speak. "They share a love that is rare," he added.

"We had that once."

He swallowed as if struggling with his own demons. "Aye."

Before she thought, she heard herself say, "How did we let it all go?"

Caleb touched her chin with his callused finger. "Sometimes what comes too easily isn't appreciated."

"It did come easily for us at first."

"As if we were meant to be together."

"Those first weeks were magic."

"Aye. Magic."

Caleb wanted to pull her into his arms and recapture the passion they'd had. Yet he held back. These last few years had been filled with so many obstacles, so much loss that he'd learned patience. Like a swimmer pulled out to sea by the riptide, he'd learned that sometimes he had to swim farther out of his way to get back to where he wanted to be.

He didn't fear what he couldn't control any longer.

So it was with Alanna.

Caleb smiled as he stared up at the bright blue sky. "Well, at least your last day here will be a beauty."

Her shoulders relaxed a fraction. She drew in a deep breath. "It is hard to believe this is the same place."

Careful not to touch her he started out toward the water. The sun sparkled on the waves like diamonds. Gulls squawked and circled overhead. "It's a fickle place. Savage and beautiful." He let out a deep breath. "We've turned the corner with the weather. I'd say we are in for fair skies for a while."

She glanced back up at the lighthouse. "Are you here alone all the time?"

"I've an assistant keeper. Likely you'll meet him today. He was on the mainland visiting his family. He'd have returned two days ago if he'd not been stranded on the mainland by the storm."

"He lives on the mainland?"

"When he's not on duty."

"Does he have a wife?"

"He's to marry in July. A nice young woman from a family in the village. April's her name."

Caleb started to walk down the beach. She fell in step beside him. This moment felt so normal that he nearly laughed.

"Why are you smiling?"

He kept his gaze on the horizon. "No drama, no passion, no fighting—just two people walking and talking to one another. Did you ever think you'd see the day between us?"

The wind teased her curls framing her face. Her eyes sparkled. "It is rather amazing."

Keeping his pace slow he pointed up ahead. "Up there where the beach curves you can find a good collection of shells."

"Really? I love shells."

"Remember the ones I brought you from the Caribbean?"

"Yes! So pink and delicate."

"These won't be as fancy, but they have their own beauty."

"I'd love to see them."

When they reached the point, as Caleb predicted, the beach was covered in shells. Laughing, Alanna hurried ahead and scanned the beach. She found a blue-black conch shell that filled the palm of her hand. "Look at this!"

Looking at her now, he'd never seen a more beautiful woman. Already the sun had added color to her pale skin and her rich blond curls, the color of sea oats, moved with the wind like thick blades of grass.

Caleb shoved his hands in his pockets for fear he'd touch her. "There's a hole on the underside of the shell."

Frowning, she turned it over and inspected the hole. "I thought it was perfect."

"It's usually the way with the shells this time of year. They don't make it in to shore without some damage."

Half expecting her to toss the shell aside, he watched her as she traced the hole with her long tapered finger. To his surprise she kept the shell.

She shrugged. "I like it better this way."

He shook his head. "There was a time when you only wanted perfect things around you. You've changed, Alanna."

She frowned. "Henry said the same thing a few weeks ago. He didn't sound very happy about it."

Henry was a fool. "My observation was meant as a compliment."

She turned the shell over and over in her hand. "I was very silly and vain. What did you ever see in me?"

He shoved out a sigh, glad they were off the topic of Henry. "You were beautiful."

She dipped her head, dropping her gaze to the sand. "Is that it?"

"You were brave and outspoken." Behind her the waves crashed and water streamed up the beach to within a foot of where they were standing. Taking her arm, he guided her away from the surf.

"Was there anything else?"

"Sensuous. Just thinking about you kept me awake well into the night. Remember the night we dined at the Capital Club?"

A warm smile curved her lips. "We danced until midnight."

He laughed. "If you can call it that. I must have stepped on your feet a half-dozen times."

She blushed. "I didn't notice. I was enjoying just being in your arms."

For a long moment they were both silent. The gulls circled, the waves crashed, and the sun warmed their skin. "It wasn't all bad, was it," Caleb said.

"No, it wasn't all bad." She traced the shell's spiral. "I should have come to you after the accident."

The muscles in his back bunched. "It doesn't matter."

She looked up at him. "It does. I wish that I could tell you that my father kept me away from you or that I was too sick to travel. But the truth was after I recovered from my miscarriage, I was scared. I was scared of the scandal. I was scared of poverty. I was scared of losing the life that I knew."

They stood inches apart from each other, but Caleb felt as if it were miles. He'd waited for this moment for years. Many times in his mind's eye he'd pictured the scene: her begging for forgiveness, him lording over her the fact that she'd been wrong. Yet, for some reason all the righteous anger melted away. "You were young. And you had just lost our child." He paused. "It will always tear at me that I'd not been there for you during that time."

"None of that was your fault."

If he'd chosen to wait until the storm passed and stayed with her, she might not have lost the baby. He'd never know for certain.

He laid his other hand on her shoulder and traced small circles on her collarbone with his thumb. "You said the early days were like magic."

She stood very still, neither moving toward him or away.

"The magic's still there, Alanna. Can you feel it?"

She went very still and for a moment she didn't speak as she gazed up into eyes. He took her hand and pressed it close to his heart. And then she laid her hand over his.

"I never wanted you more than I want you right now," he said hoarsely.

She moistened her lips. Then closing her eyes, she leaned into him, as if anticipating a kiss. He could feel her warmth curl around him.

Desire pounded in his veins. Electricity shot through his limbs. He'd not intended to kiss her yet, but the pull between them was stronger than a riptide. He lowered his head. She lifted her chin.

He wanted to wrap his arms around her waist and pull her against him. His body hardening, he wanted to feel her fingers curl into fists against his chest as she leaned into him and moaned softly.

But before their lips touched, he stopped.

Caleb fought the timeless urges that pounded in his body. He remembered too well what a passionate woman she was and how well their bodies were suited for each other. But as much as he desperately wanted to lose himself in her, he pulled back.

"We'd better get back," he said, his voice gruff.

Her eyes fluttered open. "What?"

"The sun will set soon."

Her cheeks reddening, she withdrew back. "Of course."

They'd shared passion before but it had not been enough to hold them.

This time he'd wait.

This time it would be different.

Chapter Fourteen

Alanna spent the next couple of hours alone, preparing dinner. By the time the small clock in the parlor struck six, dinner was ready. And she was in a sour mood.

Tomorrow morning, she would leave here forever. She would never see Caleb again.

Everyone was in good spirits when they sat around the table. They ate and chatted happily over the day's events. Only Caleb and Alanna were quiet. They answered questions when asked but each drifted back into their own thoughts.

Once in a while she'd get the feeling that Caleb was staring at her but when she looked up, his gaze was always averted.

"Alex," Ryan said. "Tell everyone the story about the lightkeeper in Maine. The one Captain Jamison told us about it." He looked at Thomas. "This is the darnedest story you ever did hear."

Caleb sipped his coffee as if he were half listening.

Alex finished his milk. "The way the captain told it, it was the middle of the Maine winter and the wind was like ice. The lightkeeper was on duty when he saw a ship sailing too close to the rocks. He woke his wife and lighted the bonfire always set on the beach for this kind of emergency. But they were too late and the boat crashed into the rocks. She started taking on water almost immediately."

"Those poor souls," Debra said. "I know the feeling well. Terrifying."

Alanna didn't want to listen to the story. Her memories of her near-drowning were too fresh.

As if sensing her shift in mood, Caleb set his cup down. He focused on Alex. "Boy, I'm in no mood for sad tales."

Ryan shook his head. "It ain't sad."

Alex waited for Caleb's nod before he continued. "The keeper and his wife started running along the beach, looking for survivors and debris. There were already beams and broken cargo boxes everywhere. But there weren't one survivor."

"Why didn't he sail out to save them," Thomas asked. "Just as Captain Pitt saved us."

"Most keepers don't go into the heavy surf.

Most just don't have the strength to take a boat into the surf.''

Thomas frowned, nodded but said nothing.

"Listen to this," Ryan said. "You won't believe—"

"Shh," Alex said. "It's my story to tell."

"Then get on with it," Ryan said.

Alex's gaze shifted between Alanna, Debra and Thomas. "Anyway, the keeper was running up the beach when he saw something in the surf. In the dark it looked like a body so he ran for it. But when he got there he found it weren't nothing but a feather mattress wrapped up like a jellyroll.

"The keeper was disappointed. Here he was freezing. His fingers were numb and all he got for his trouble was a mattress. But he went ahead and dragged the mattress up to the beach.''

Ryan, unable to contain his excitement said, "That's when he see the cord banded around the mattress. So he pulls out his pocket knife and slashes the rope.''

"It unwound," Alex said quickly. "And in the center was a wooden wine box.''

Caleb leaned forward, but remained silent.

Alanna too found she couldn't resist the story. "What was in the box?''

"A baby!" Ryan said.

Alex frowned at him. "A baby boy it turned out."

Debra pressed her hand to her lips. "Was he alive?"

"Crying and screaming like the banshees was on his tail, but he was right as rain," Alex said.

Alanna felt her stomach clench. "He must have been freezing."

"There wasn't a drop of water on him," Alex said. "Looked to be a newborn, not more than five days old. And there weren't a drop of water on him."

"He came from the wreck," Debra asked.

Alex nodded. "Yes, ma'am. There was a note inside the box. Said, Lord protect my baby, Elijah."

"What a miracle," Debra said. She took Thomas's hand and squeezed it.

"What happened to the mother and the ship," Alanna asked.

"Minutes after they started toward the house, the ship started to break apart. All was lost," Alex said.

Everyone around the table went silent.

Uneasy, Alanna rose and moved to the stove. That poor woman, she thought. "The sea brought so much misery."

"Well," Ryan said. "Have you heard the story

about the ship that wrecked off San Francisco? It was loaded with animals from South America. I heard tell a dozen monkeys floated to shore on a piece of wreckage. The lightkeeper never did catch them. Some say you can still hear the monkeys squeaking in the trees to this day.''

Alanna and the others laughed, Caleb included. She pictured Caleb trying to herd a pack of monkeys and despite her sour mood smiled.

When the laughter died down, Debra rose. ''Alanna, let me help you with these dishes.''

Alanna took the platter Debra had lifted from the table. ''I won't hear of it. You must sit down.''

She picked up another plate and carried it to the sink. She pumped cold water into the basin. ''Now off to the parlor with you. You should be resting. This is a delicate time for you.''

Caleb met her gaze and frowned. She could almost read his mind. He was trying to picture her pregnant with their child.

He paused a moment before he seemed to trust his voice. ''There's a basin in the storage closet. I'll haul it in along with water from the barrels. The stove is hot so it shouldn't take more than an hour for the water to heat.''

Alanna felt her heart leap. A hot bath! Until now she'd managed with a wash cloth and a basin filled with cold water. "Do you mean it? If it's too much trouble I can wait until we go into town tomorrow. I'm sure Mr. Sloan will allow me to use one of his rooms."

Pleased by her reaction, he smiled. "No trouble at all, Alanna."

"That would be such luxury." Her voice sounded husky.

"It's not a grand tub like you'd have found in your father's house. You won't be able to stretch your legs."

"If the water is hot and I can wash the salt from my hair, I don't care if it's fancy or not." Excited, she squeezed his hand. "This is the greatest gift you could have given me."

He touched a curl hanging loose from her ponytail. Her breathing grew shallow, anxious.

"Happy to help," he said finally.

As promised, Caleb delivered the tub and set it near the stove in the kitchen. It took him half an hour to haul the water inside. Another hour and a half passed before the water heated. With each passing minute, Alanna's anticipation grew.

She'd found soaps. A pale brown, the soaps weren't the exotic French soaps she'd once favored, but they would do. She'd also rounded up a clean towel.

She skimmed her hand over the warm water's surface. Such a simple pleasure but she had never been more excited. She intended to savor every moment.

Unpinning her braid, she let it fall down her back. Untying the piece of string at the bottom of the braid, she loosened the hair. Her hair was so dirty. It lacked shine and was flat.

She reached for her belted robe. This was going to be good.

"Oh my heavens," Debra said. "Is that a bath?"

Alanna turned, nodding. "It sure is." It struck her that Debra looked pale. "And it's for you."

Debra eyed her skeptically. "This bath is not for me. *You* were about to get in."

Alanna walked over to Debra. "I will take one after you. You need a bath."

Debra shook her head. "Absolutely not. You have done far too much for me."

Alanna stepped back and turned toward the back door. "You better hurry, the water is just right."

Tears streamed down Debra's face. "Are you sure?"

"Very." The look of joy on the young woman's face had Alanna smiling as she strolled outside.

Though the sun had gone down, the air had turned warm and there was a gentle breeze. Next to the porch stood a barrel. She took a seat and stared up into the cloudless sky. Countless stars winked at her.

She heard footsteps in the dirt and turned. Caleb stepped out of the shadows. "What are you doing here? I thought you'd be in the tub."

"Debra is going first."

He studied her a moment as if he couldn't quite figure her out. "I made the bath for you."

"It was a wonderful gift. Debra just looked as if she needed it more than me." She drew in a deep breath, savoring the salt air. She felt his gaze on her. "There must be a million stars tonight."

"Aye."

"They're so much brighter out here than in town."

He shoved his hands in his pockets. "Would you like to see them from the crow's nest?"

"At the top of the lighthouse?" Excitement bubbled in her voice.

He held out his hand to her. "The very same."

She hesitated then laid her hand in his. Strong fingers wrapped round her hand. Suddenly, she felt like a schoolgirl. "Lead the way."

They crossed the yard toward the twenty-foot tall granite-and-brick base of the lighthouse. The lighthouse stretched toward the night sky, its beacon flashing steady and bright.

Caleb opened the door and they entered the circular base. He lit two lanterns and handed her one. He nodded toward a spiral staircase. ''Follow me.''

He started up the stairs with the confidence of a man who had climbed these steps hundreds of times. She doubted he needed the lantern.

At first, she matched his pace but after a few dozen steps, she began to breathe harder and her legs ached. Caleb hadn't broken his stride. She was able to push through her discomfort at first, but with each step her feet grew heavier.

Finally, she stopped. ''I—I need a moment.''

He stopped and, turning, held up his lantern. ''The first time I climbed these steps I thought my heart would explode.''

''My heart exploded a dozen steps ago,'' she said, wheezing.

He chuckled and sat down on a step. ''There's no rush.''

She hated showing weakness so she remained standing. ''Maybe a minute.'' She glanced up the winding spiral stairwell. It seemed to go on and on forever.

''How many times a day do you climb these steps?''

"Five or six."

Moistening dry lips she glanced over the railing down toward the base. Her head spun. "Oh my, we are up high."

"Wait until you get to the top."

Heights had never been a favorite of hers. If it was with anyone else but Caleb she'd have turned around. "How high up is this lighthouse?"

"262 steps." His gaze dropped to her white-knuckle grip on the railing.

"You do this every day?" The concept baffled her.

"Aye. And in the old days, with a can of oil strapped to my back." He studied her flushed cheeks. "Let's rest for a minute."

Alanna didn't have the breath to argue. She sat down on the metal steps grateful for the respite. "The old days. Alex said your family was from here."

He nodded slowly. "Born on this very island."

She stared at him with fresh eyes. "Why didn't you ever tell me?"

He shrugged. "At the time, I never planned to return and the past simply didn't matter."

Guilt tugged at her. "You knew everything about me. Yet, I realize now I knew next to nothing about you. I'm sorry."

"Why?"

"I should have asked. I should have known more about your past." She remembered the journal entry: *Keeper Pitt died today.* "The boys told me your father was a Keeper here."

"Yes." He glanced up the stairwell. "We've about seventy-five steps to go. Can you make it or do you want to turn back?"

She realized the subject of his father was sensitive. There'd been a time when she'd have pried and prodded until she got all the details. "And miss the view from the top? Never."

Smiling, he rose slowly. "You always were stubborn."

She'd have argued the point if she could have spared the breath. Concentrating on placing one foot in front of the other, she climbed the stairs.

When they reached the top she collapsed against the brick. "I'll never make it back down."

He chuckled. "Yes, you will. The hard part is over. Now it's time to enjoy the view."

Exhausted she closed her eyes and let her head fall forward. "My eyes are too tired to focus."

Alanna was certain her lungs would explode. Caleb wasn't even winded.

Before them was a metal door. Caleb pulled a ring of metal keys from his pocket and unlocked the door. "This door keeps the gusts of wind from extinguishing the light."

Alanna sucked in another breath. She nodded, refusing to spare precious air to speak.

He smiled. "Just a few more steps."

"More?" She shook her head. "Why don't you just tell me about it."

Chuckling, he placed his hand under her elbow. His fingers felt strong and without really questioning why, she leaned into him. "Seven steps."

She started to follow him. "Might as well be seven thousand."

"You can make it." He coaxed her up the small winding staircase.

With his help, this last climb seemed easy. "Where are we going?"

"The watch room."

The watch room was just steps below the lens room. The lantern above turned steadily, flashing its warning light to all in the Atlantic.

Alanna looked up the small spiral staircase to the room above, alight with the beacon. She marveled at the size of the room. "How does it move?"

Caleb followed her gaze to the beacon. "There's a weight. I crank it to the top each evening. As it slowly drops it turns the gears and causes the lens to rotate."

The enormity of Caleb's responsibilities humbled her. "Must you do it every day?"

"Every day." He placed his hand in the small of her back and nodded toward an iron door. "The balcony is through there."

She glanced up one last time toward the lens room and then allowed him to guide her outside.

The night view was breathtaking. The stars gleamed with unusual brightness and freckled the night sky. The breeze was gentle and the crash of the waves roared in the distance. The giant lantern light rotated above them.

"It's beautiful," she breathed. Again, she got a glimpse of how wondrous this place could be. A part of her envied Caleb. This could be a magical place.

Caleb leaned close to her and stretched out his arm toward the coast. "See that flicker on the horizon?"

Her gaze followed the length of his arm. There was a light. It blinked off and then blinked on.

"It's the Bodie Lighthouse. She stands about sixty miles down the coast from here. Beyond Bodie, there's the Hatteras Lighthouse. Beyond that, Cape Fear."

She leaned against him, content to savor his warmth and the evening breeze. The sound of frogs and katydids crooned in the distant marshes.

An animal called out to the night, its sound sad and lonely. "What's that?"

He wrapped his arm around her. "It's called chuck-wills widows. Some say it sounds like the cry of lost souls."

She listened to the sad cry. The beacon above flashed brilliantly and then it was dark again. Suddenly, an unbearable weight settled on her shoulders as she thought about a life without Caleb. "Lost souls. That is what we are."

He placed his hands on her shoulders. He leaned his face forward so that his lips were next to her ear. He waited for the light to flash and the darkness to return before he spoke. "We don't have to be. Stay here with me."

"It's not that simple."

His fingers tightened. "It is that simple."

"We don't belong together anymore. Our lives don't fit anymore." She fought the seductive pull of his body.

Turning, she faced him. The light beacon flashed on his face, now stiff with emotion. Her throat tightened with unshed tears. "I'm sorry."

Unable to bear the look of pain on his face, she turned and went back into the watch room. He didn't follow. Tears choked her throat as she grabbed a lantern and hurried down the stairs.

* * *

Caleb's fingers gripped the wrought-iron fence around the crow's nest. Alanna's descending steps mingled with the crash of the wave.

A small smile curved the edge of his lips. "You are wrong, Alanna. We do belong together."

Chapter Fifteen

Alanna decided the boat ride across the sound was painfully fast. The Randalls rode in another dory with Ryan and Alex on the oars. She sat in a boat alone with Caleb.

Freshly bathed and wearing the dress she'd mended, she looked more like herself. Her blond hair, tied back in a long braid, had regained its luster. Her skin felt smooth and clean. Three days ago, she would have sold her soul for this moment. Now the idea of leaving tore at her.

She and Caleb had not spoken more than six words since their trip up into the lighthouse last night. Each was lost in their thoughts.

She was keenly aware of him. His presence. His scent. The even sound of his breathing.

"There are circles under your eyes," Caleb said as he dug the oars into the water.

''I didn't sleep well last night.'' He'd spent the night in the lighthouse as she now knew he often did while on duty so she'd had his room to herself. But lying in his bed, surrounded by everything that was his, had made sleep impossible.

''You never could sleep when you were worried. What is it this time?'' There was an edge to his voice.

''Nothing.'' What wasn't she worried about? Leaving him, facing Henry, or trying to go back to her old life as if these last few days hadn't happened.

''You're going to miss me.''

She stiffened, but she did not turn around. Dear Lord, she was going to miss him terribly.

Silent, she stared at Easton. When they'd set out from the barrier, it had started as a thin line on the horizon. Now it was fully in focus.

Just days ago, the town had seemed so lifeless, bleached gray by the blistering sun and wind. To her surprise, the sunshine had transformed the town. On this warm spring morning, Easton was filled with color. Against an azure sky, the brightly hued shutters, the carts filled with fish and vegetables brought the place alive. She heard children's laughter and dogs barking. The docks that had been deserted when she'd departed were now filled with villagers who had shed their thick, dark capes.

Several people on the dock spotted their dory. Many waved a greeting.

From the crowd, stepped Sloan. He still wore a stained apron as he had a few days before, but this time he was smiling.

Alanna almost feared meeting these people. Something deep inside her told her she just might like them.

Caleb moored the boat alongside the dock and tossed a rope line up to Sloan.

Sloan caught the rope easily and tied it to a metal ring attached to the dock. "I see you weathered the storm."

"I could say the same for you."

Laughing, the barkeeper's gaze pinned Alanna briefly then shifted to the Randalls, Alex and Ryan. "Looks like you fished your share out of the drink these last few days."

Caleb nodded. "You know Alex and Ryan."

Sloan shook his head as the boys tied their boat to the pier. "You two had best go find your mothers. Once they get over the shock of seeing you alive, they're going to gut you like fish."

Alex groaned. "I'll never hear the end of this."

Caleb laid his oars down in the bottom of his boat. "Good."

Sloan shifted his attention back to Caleb. "When Crowley came back without the woman, I figured she'd drowned."

Caleb tensed. "Aye, I've been meaning to have a talk with him."

"He took off as soon as the weather cleared. I doubt he'll be back any time soon." Sloan looked at Alanna. "I got your bag from Crowley. It's at my inn."

Alanna had given up the bag as lost forever. Yet the discovery that it had been retrieved didn't excite her as she'd first thought. She rose and reached for the ladder built into the side of the pier. "That's very kind of you, Mr. Sloan."

He squinted and studied her. "You look different."

"Plainer and duller no doubt," she said trying to keep her voice light. "I retrieved this dress from a chest in Caleb's cottage."

Sloan's eyes burned with a keen intensity. "No, I'd say you look a sight better. All that nonsense you wore was a bit of a distraction."

Alanna climbed up the ladder to the dock. "I'll take that as a compliment."

Sloan sucked in his belly a fraction. "Aye, it's a compliment."

Ryan and Alex scrambled up the ladder. The boys extended their hands to Thomas as he climbed the ladder. "Thanks, boys." He leaned down and helped guide Debra up the ladder. He then extended his hand to Sloan. "Sir, I am Thomas Randall and this is my wife, Debra."

Sloan took the man's hand. "Pleasure. I reckon you hail from the *Annabelle Lee*."

"That's right."

"I heard from some of the villagers who was on her late yesterday," Sloan said. "She's all but broken up now."

Debra drew in a deep breath of air. She looked pale and unsteady. "I have never been more glad to be on dry land. I doubt I will ever get on a boat again."

Thomas frowned as he looked down at his wife. "Debra, are you feeling all right?"

"Very tired and a bit seasick."

Caleb climbed up to the pier. "Sloan runs a good inn. It's clean and a good place for you to rest before the morning stage. I'll talk with some of the men in town and see about a cart for your belongings."

Thomas extended his hand to Caleb. "We cannot thank you enough."

Caleb shook his hand. "It was a pleasure."

Debra smiled up at Caleb. "Mr. Pitt, thank you." She hugged Alanna. "It was a pleasure to meet you. I will never forget you or your husband.''

Sloan lifted a brow and met Caleb's gaze. "Husband?"

Ryan nudged Alex with his elbow. "Guess you didn't hear, Mr. Sloan. Caleb got himself married."

Sloan lifted an eyebrow. "That so?"

Caleb shoved out a breath. "I'll fill in the details later."

Sloan's gaze darted between Alanna and Caleb. "Now this is a tale I would not miss for the world."

Caleb felt the villagers' stares as he and Alanna moved down the muddy main street. He was a man who kept his own counsel but there were few secrets in Easton. Most knew something of his time in Virginia and all knew there'd been a woman in his past. He could almost hear the questions dancing about in everyone's heads.

Who is she? Is she the one? Did he really marry her?

In Richmond after the accident, he couldn't have given a tinker's damn what people had thought about him. His mistakes were between him and the families who'd lost someone on the *Intrepid*. No one else had mattered.

But the people in Easton were different. They were family. This was his home. Many of these people were kin. And he wanted them to like Alanna.

"People are staring," Alanna muttered as they made their way down the sandy road toward the village.

He pressed his hand into the small of her back and guided her to the weathered boardwalk. "Strangers always stir the pot in Easton."

"Do you think Alex and Ryan have been talking?"

"Oh, yes."

An old woman on the street corner—Ida Watson—stared at them with uncensored curiosity. She wore a black skirt and blouse and a crocheted shawl on her thin shoulders. He'd known her since he was six and she'd caught him stealing green apples from the tree in her backyard. The old woman had marched him straight to his father and the two agreed that Caleb would pick twenty bushels of apples for Ida as punishment. He'd shown up at her house the next day and worked all morning in the hot sun. Ida's mood had softened when she'd seen how hard he'd worked and she'd brought him lemonade and cookies.

Squinting, her face looked as wrinkled as a

sun-baked apple. "Caleb Pitt," Ida squawked. "Who's that woman on your arm?"

Caleb didn't hesitate. "This is Alanna."

"Some say she's your wife."

Caleb lifted an eyebrow. "Is that what they're saying?"

Ida looked at Alanna. "Are you married to this man or not?" Ida demanded.

He felt Alanna stiffen. He half expected her to lie her way out of this one, but she said, "Not exactly."

Ida snorted. "What the devil does that mean? Either you is married or you ain't. Sorta like a little pregnant."

Alanna blushed. "I suppose then we're not—"

"We'll talk later, Ida," Caleb interrupted. "You know if the stage has arrived yet?"

Ida nodded. "About ten minutes ago."

The old woman wasn't happy. She wanted more information out of Caleb but she knew he gave answers only when he was good and ready.

"See you two at the auction," Ida grumbled.

After the old woman was out of earshot, Alanna shoved out a sigh. "This is not good."

"What?"

She shook her head. "Alex and Ryan have told everyone that we are married."

He shrugged. "You're the one that started this farce."

She glared up at him, a grin plastered on her face. "I never thought it would go this far. The entire town is whispering about us."

"That's about right."

She stopped dead in her tracks. "I know what you're thinking. It wasn't an impulsive decision. The situation arose and I had to think fast."

He liked the way her cheeks flushed when she got angry. "You could have told the truth. In fact you can go to Debra now and tell her."

She frowned. "I have to tell Debra the truth. I owe her that much. I'm sure she'll understand."

He could read her mind. "And it no longer matters if she agrees to keep your secret or not."

"What do you mean?"

"Don't you think Henry's figured out something is wrong? You're two days overdue and sunburned. I know Henry can be a bit slow, but he's going to figure out where you've been."

"Maybe he won't."

"Henry lives in a very orderly world, Alanna. You can set your watch by him."

Her brow knotted. "He can be flexible."

"Tell me, does he still have lunch at the Capital Club on Fridays, sit in the third pew at the Presbyterian Church and drink precisely one and a half cups of sherry after dinner?''

''We all have our habits.''

''Henry can't stand disorder. Once he discovers you are not where he left you, he'll move heaven and earth to put things back in their proper place.''

''I'll make it up to him. I'll start wearing a watch so that I can be on time for every event.''

Caleb heard the hint of desperation in her voice. She was trying to convince herself as much as him. ''It's your nature not to bend to routine. No matter how much money you'll have access to as his wife, you'll go mad if you force yourself to live the life he's mapped out for you.''

''He loves me,'' she whispered.

''Aye, he just might. But that doesn't mean he's good for you.''

She arched an eyebrow. ''So, I suppose you know what's good for me?''

He brushed a curl from her forehead. ''Aye, I do. Me.''

Her shoulders slumped. ''Caleb, please. I thought we agreed you are better off without me.''

''You agreed, not me.''

''Don't make this hard for me.''

"Sorry. My days of playing fair are over. I'll do what it takes to convince you to stay."

"I don't belong here."

"Why do you keep saying that?" he challenged. "Do you hate it here that much?"

Her gaze scanned the town. "It's not that. This town is lovely. But I'm from a different world. And as much as I enjoy it here today, what's going to happen if things get hard." She squeezed his hand. "I couldn't bear to let you down again."

He raised her hand to his lips and kissed her. "You won't."

Her eyes reflected a mixture of pleasure and fear. "I can't take that risk."

"Since when were you afraid of risk?"

"Since now." She tried to pull her hands free. "I need to go to the inn and get my bag. I can wait there for the morning coach."

Caleb didn't release her hand. He'd meant what he'd said. He'd move the heavens to keep her. But despite the growing fear inside him that he could lose her, he kept his voice light. "And miss the auction? You've got to see it."

"That's all right."

Still holding her hand, he started to walk down the street toward Hudson's Docks, where the auctions were always held. "It's scheduled for two o'clock. There's always good food and music. With the sun shining as it is today, it'll be a fun time.''

''I shouldn't go.''

''Why not?''

''We should say our goodbyes now.''

His insides clenched at the thought of her leaving. ''There is time for that tomorrow.''

She had to hurry her pace to keep up with his. ''I think I've stirred up enough gossip and trouble in your life.''

''Gossip has never bothered me. And I like your kind of trouble.''

Her face reflected her fear and longing. ''Caleb, this isn't a good idea.''

''Tomorrow's a long way off, Alanna,'' he said. ''And this day is too nice to waste sitting in a dark inn. Come with me to the auction.'' He cocked an eyebrow. ''What do you have to lose?''

She shoved out a sigh. ''Everything.''

Laughter rumbled in his chest.

Alanna didn't want to have fun.

But soon, she found herself enjoying the lively crowd that had turned the auction of the *Nicholas B.,* a schooner that had sunk off the coast last month, into a celebration. Many families had brought food and picnic blankets. A fiddler played lively tunes between bids and the children ran around.

The villagers bid widely on a variety of items from steamer trucks, lanterns, ropes and furniture. Two sailors got into a heated bidding over a carved mermaid, which had adorned the front of the vessel. The final bid was twenty-four dollars.

Across the crowd she saw Debra and Thomas. The two were standing side by side, holding hands. Debra looked up into Thomas's eyes. He cupped his hand to her round belly. They shared so much love; it made Alanna's heart ache.

Alanna was very aware of Caleb. He stood next to her, greeting everyone who approached. Sloan brought them both ale. They talked of the weather and the price of items up for sale. A cobbler told Caleb his new boots were ready. A fisherman thanked him for the warning last week of the weather—because of Caleb's warning the fisherman had dry-docked his boats and they'd not been damaged by the storm.

In Easton, Caleb was a different man. Relaxed and at peace, he smiled and even laughed. His laugh was rich and deep and it struck her she'd never heard him laugh before. Yes, he'd smiled and teased her in the old days, but she'd never seen him toss back his head and laugh. He looked years younger.

She noticed the young girls staring at Caleb and then at her. They were clearly disappointed that he'd gotten "married." Soon however, they would learn that he was still quite eligible.

Jealousy jolted her system. He likely would end up marrying one of them one day.

Caleb's wife would be an active partner, helping manage the lighthouse and assisting with rescues. The work would likely be backbreaking at times. The days would not be full of social engagements but quiet and, yes, sometimes lonely.

Alanna envied the woman that would one day be Caleb's wife.

"Captain Pitt!" A boy who looked little more than six ran up to Caleb. The child wore oversize boots, pants that hit him midcalf and a white shirt covered with food stains. Freckles covered his face. "You said you'd race me at the next auction."

Caleb, his eyes dancing, looked down at the boy. "Where are your manners, John? There's a lady present."

The boy shot Alanna a quick glance. "Sorry, ma'am, but he promised me a race."

Alanna nodded, trying to look serious. "Well, a promise is a promise. Don't let me keep you."

Caleb reached in his pocket and pulled out a

white handkerchief. "We'll need an official starter. Alanna?"

"Me?"

"We want this race to be fair," Caleb said, his tone serious.

Alanna bit back a smile. "Of course."

Her fingers brushed his when she took the handkerchief and for a moment she imagined electricity shooting up her fingertips. She cleared her throat. "Where would you gentlemen like to race?"

"What do you think, John?" Caleb said.

The boy nodded toward the field next to the cemetery surrounded by a wrought-iron fence. "There's a patch of grass over there. That should do."

"Lead the way, sir," Caleb said.

The boy, as if he were a general leading an army, led the way. "You ain't gonna beat me this time. I've been practicing."

"I'm mighty fast," Caleb said, his voice serious. "And I have been practicing, too."

Alanna walked a step behind the two and couldn't help but smile as she watched John try to match Caleb's swagger. The boy even shoved his left hand in his pocket like Caleb.

When they reached the fence, Alanna looked to John. "Where should I stand?"

He glanced up at Caleb who nodded for him to answer. "Right there would be fine. Me and the captain are going to the edge of the fence. You hold up the white flag, then say ready, set, go."

"Yes, sir."

Caleb glanced back at her and winked. Her heart melted and she flashed him a bright smile. His eyes darkened and for a moment, she glimpsed something dark and primitive that made her knees go weak with wanting.

At twenty paces, John said, "Stop right here, Caleb. This is far enough."

"Will do." Caleb lined up with the boy. "Ready, Alanna?"

Alanna raised the handkerchief high above her head. "Ready?"

John's lips were pursed with concentration. Caleb rubbed his hands down his thighs and leaned forward.

"Set," Alanna shouted. She waited an extra beat then shouted, "Go."

John took off like a bullet. Pumping his arms, he moved his legs as quickly as he could. Caleb made a good bit of stomping noise and though his long legs could easily have eaten up the twenty paces in no time, he lagged behind the boy about a foot.

"I'm gonna beat you," Caleb shouted.

''No, you ain't.''

John crossed the finish line with Caleb right on his heels. The boy jumped up and down, thrilled by his victory, while Caleb bent forward his hands on his knees as if he were trying to catch his breath.

Alanna smothered a grin. This show of Caleb's was for John's benefit. Today Caleb had rowed in the surfboat full of the Randalls' furniture and he'd barely been winded. ''Mr. Pitt, I thought you ran faster than that.''

He straightened slowly. ''I must be slowing with age.''

John, breathing hard, extended his hand to Caleb. ''That was a fine effort.''

Alanna tried to imagine Henry tossing off his coat and loosening his tie to race a child. She couldn't picture him ever doing such a thing.

Caleb nodded, all serious as he dug in his pocket and pulled out a quarter. ''I believe the deal was for two bits.''

John stared at the money in Caleb's palm. His eyes danced with excitement. ''I really won that?''

Caleb handed the boy the money. ''Fair and square.''

''This is great!'' John said, his excitement bubbling over. ''Wait until I show Ma.''

"Run on then and show her."

The air was warm, the wind soft and she was very aware of Caleb next to her as they watched John run back toward the crowd. In his eyes, she read happiness and sadness.

"He's a good boy," she said.

Caleb tore his gaze from John. "Aye."

"How do you know him?"

Taking her elbow in hand, he started to walk with her away from the crowd. "His father served with me on the *Intrepid*. He died in the accident."

Twenty-three men had died in the accident but she'd never thought about the people left behind. How many other children had lost fathers? How many women had lost sons or husbands? So consumed about how the accident had affected her life, she'd never stopped to think about the families of the lost men. Sadness and guilt roughed her voice. "How did John end up in Easton?"

This close, she noted the crow's feet at his eyes.

"I knew his mother needed a job. I knew Sloan needed a cook."

He spoke so matter-of-factly, but the enormity of what he'd done wasn't lost on her. His compassion touched her. She remembered how loyal Caleb's men had been to him. "How many other families have you helped?"

His fingers tightened on her elbow. For a moment, she thought he wouldn't answer. "A dozen."

She remembered what Alex had said about Caleb's trip to Virginia. "That's why you went to Virginia last month."

He guided her toward a large oak tree next to the cemetery's fence. He shoved out a sigh. "I made a small fortune during the years I worked for your father. Unlike him, I saved what I'd earned, so after the accident, I had plenty of money to see me through."

She didn't speak. He was a man who could bargain or negotiate better than anyone, but speaking of emotions had always been hard for him.

"I've spent the last of my savings last month, settling the debts of my first mate's mother."

Again, she compared Henry to Caleb and again Henry fell short. Henry had moments of generosity, but he gave when it was easy to give. He never inconvenienced himself for anyone, not even her.

In that moment, she knew no matter what happened here today, she'd not marry Henry. Yes, he offered safety and security but both seemed paltry in comparison to Caleb's honor and kindness.

"That was very kind and generous of you," she said.

Caleb traced the freshly painted finial on the iron gate. ''Some would say I was easing my guilt with money. Money in exchange for a clear conscience.'' He nodded. ''And I will admit, I want the guilt to go away. But no amount of money I spend will ever turn back the clock or bring those men back to their families.''

She laid her hand on his arm. Tension radiated from every sinew. ''Your men understood the risks, Caleb.''

''I should have died with them.'' His voice was dark, savage.

''No!'' The thought of him dead was unbearable and it took a moment for her emotions to steady.

He stared down at her as if touched by the force of her emotion.

The weight of the past bore down on them both and for a long time they were silent. The wind rustled through the leaves of the trees and she stared past him into the cemetery. Atop one gravestone sat a winged angel.

Alanna wasn't sure if she touched Caleb first or if he reached for her first. But when their fingertips brushed, fire shot through her veins. Her fingers interlocked with his. ''Lord, but it feels right to touch you. I know I shouldn't but I can't seem to stop.''

He sucked in a ragged breath. "Then don't."

She moved a step closer. Her chest brushed his. Her nipples hardened.

He bent his head, ready to kiss her. As wrong as she was for wanting the forbidden, she wanted him to kiss her and take her in his arms.

Rising up on tiptoe, she wrapped her arms around his shoulders. Curling her fingers through his dark hair, she savored the feel of him. She'd forgotten just how right it felt to be in his arms.

Nothing would make her deny this moment.

"Alanna!"

Henry.

Alanna turned and discovered Henry striding toward her. His expression was murderous.

Chapter Sixteen

Immediately, Alanna stepped back from Caleb. She felt the blood drain from her face. "Henry!"

Henry's blond hair billowed in the breeze as he moved through the throng of people toward her. Despite the heat, he wore a black wool suit, fresh collar and cuffs and black polished boots that reflected the sun. His hands were manicured, and he wore a gold signet ring on his left pinky. Meticulously dressed as always.

Alanna could feel Caleb tense but he said nothing. He stood rigidly behind her, his fingers fisted.

"How did you find me?" she asked.

Henry stopped in front of them. His gaze shifted to Caleb and his lips flattened into a thin line. "You left a trail anyone could have followed." Manicured fingers tugged at the edge of his vest. "Alanna, do you have any idea what it felt like to find you'd simply left Richmond alone?''

The reproach in his voice had her raising her chin. "I'm sorry if I worried you. That was not my intent, honestly."

"You never mean to cause trouble, do you?" Henry said, his voice biting.

Caleb stood directly behind Alanna. "Strathmore, watch the tone."

Henry kept his gaze on Alanna. "What are you doing with *him?*" He spoke as if Caleb wasn't there. "Hasn't he done enough damage to your life?"

Alanna refused to take the bait. She returned to her original question. "How did you find me, Henry?"

"I went to your attorney. When I told him you hadn't been seen in a week, he was only too happy to tell me where you'd gone."

"You shouldn't have been so hard on Mr. Piper. He had been a good friend to me."

"Friends don't allow ladies to travel unescorted."

Only three years older than she, Henry acted as if he were twenty years her senior. Had he always been so staid?

Caleb took hold of Alanna's arm, the move

purely masculine. He was sending Henry a clear message. *Mine.* "Henry, you and I need to talk."

Henry reached in his vest pocket and pulled out a shiny gold watch. He clicked it open, checked the time then replaced it in his pocket. "Pitt, you are a waste of my time."

The muscle in Caleb's jaw jumped. "Make the time."

Danger laced Caleb's voice. Henry clearly heard it. He took a step back and his face paled. "Alanna and I have to leave now if we're to catch the morning steamer from Coinjock Bay to Norfolk."

Alanna felt the tension radiating from Caleb. "Let me talk to Henry."

Caleb's jaw tightened. "I'm not leaving you alone with him."

"It'll be all right. I owe him an explanation. I won't hide from conflict this time."

Caleb stood silent for a moment staring at her. Finally, he nodded. "I'll be at the inn." He glared at Henry, and then strode away.

Alanna watched him go. Only when he'd disappeared out of sight into the crowd did she look at Henry. "I should have discussed my trip with you but I was afraid you'd try and stop me."

Henry let out the breath he'd been holding. Some of his ire returned. "Of course I would have stopped you. If word of this little *jaunt* were to get out you'd be the laughingstock of town. No decent person would accept you again." He shook his head. "Pitt is a pariah in polite circles."

A bitter taste settled in her mouth. "Ah, the same circles that turned their backs on me after Father died?"

Henry tugged his vest down. "Alanna, you're not thinking clearly."

"Maybe I am." Her friends had all but deserted her when news of her father's suicide became known. Abruptly, she wondered why she'd been in such a hurry to return to that life.

Henry lowered his voice. "Do you know the lengths I had to go to to cover this up? Thanks to me everyone now believes you are still at your aunt's in Washington."

The muscles in her stomach coiled tight. "You didn't have to do that, Henry."

Henry's face softened and he laid his hands on her shoulders. "Of course I did. I love you, Alanna. I don't want you to be hurt by vicious gossip." He glanced down at her simple dress. "Where on earth did you find that dress? If any one of our friends was to see you now, they'd be appalled. Dear God, you look like a half-drowned cat."

"It was a castoff. My clothes were lost when I was crossing the sound to the barrier island."

Henry hissed in a breath. "You went to the lighthouse?"

Disgust dripped from his words. "Yes."

He pulled in several deep breaths then forced a smile. "Why did you do such a foolish thing?"

"Remember the box Father left Caleb? I came to deliver it."

"Lord Almighty, Alanna. Any reasonable woman would have used a messenger or better yet tossed the damn box in the trash."

"I couldn't do that," she said softly.

Henry shook his head, as if staring at a small child. "You could have drowned."

"I nearly did drown. Caleb saved me."

The import of her words seemed to pass over his head. "Well, the thing that is important now is that you are safe."

"Yes."

"And you're in luck. I've a friend who has a house in Waverly. They are away and I'm sure we can stop long enough to get you cleaned up and into decent clothes. No one will be the wiser." He took her by the hand. "The stage I hired is waiting."

Alanna's stomach clenched. She dreaded what needed to be said. "I'm not going, Henry."

He shook his head as if he hadn't heard correctly. "What do you mean you're not going?"

"I want to stay here."

He patted her hand. "You haven't thought this through."

A wave of calm warmed her limbs. It felt so good to know what she wanted. It was so obvious now; she wondered why she'd not seen it before. "I have."

"A week ago, I asked you to marry me. I was certain your doubts would pass and you'd say yes. And now you want to live in this godforsaken place. What's come over you?"

"I don't know, exactly. I just know that it feels right."

"It *feels* right." His laugh was bitter. "That's rich, Alanna."

Tipping her chin up she kept her voice even. "It's not funny, Henry."

"Are you ever going to grow up?"

She straightened her shoulders. "I think that I finally have."

"If I did everything I *felt* like doing, I certainly wouldn't be here now."

"I didn't ask you to come."

"Alanna, since I was in short pants, my parents talked about nothing but us marrying. And we would have been now if not for Caleb Pitt."

"I fell in love with him."

The import of those simply spoken words rocked her to her very core. *She was in love with Caleb.*

Only with great effort was she able to refocus on Henry. "I'm sorry, what did you say?"

Annoyed, he cleared his throat. "Don't you remember how terrible those days were for you after the accident. You weren't yourself for months. And then your father's death."

Those days seemed like a distant bad dream. For the first time in years, she felt free of them. "The only mistake I made was that I didn't stand by him."

"He's a washed-up sea captain, Alanna. He's lost his nerve. He'll never pilot his own ship again."

She almost laughed. "Caleb is the bravest man I know."

"Brave? The man ran from Richmond with his tail stuck between his legs."

She stepped back. "I've heard enough, Henry."

"Alanna, you need to get away from this place. You need perspective."

"I finally have it, Henry."

Henry leaned toward her. His soft features had hardened in a way she'd never seen before. "Oba-

diah was right to burn Caleb's letter. He was right
to keep you two apart until you could get control
of yourself.''

Stunned, she could only stare at him for a moment. ''You knew about Caleb's letters?''

''I read them.''

Tears of outrage burned her eyes. ''You had no
right.''

''You weren't yourself in those days. Someone
had to look out for you.''

Her anger exploded. ''How dare you!''

''Alanna, I did it for your own good. I needed
to know what I was up against. I feared you'd go
chasing after him if you read his mush. The man
has some kind of hold on you.''

All these years, and she didn't know Henry at
all.

Henry swept his hand toward the village.
''Case in point. We are here now because you
couldn't send some foolish box by courier.''

Alanna wondered now how she could ever have
cared for him. ''I'm staying.''

''So we're back to that again? Look, I'm running out of patience.''

''That's your affair. But I'm staying.'' She'd
had enough and stared to walk away from him.

He grabbed her arm. His fingers bit into her

flesh. "If you don't leave with me now, we are done. I won't clean up any more of your messes."

She jerked her arm away. "So be it."

"He doesn't love you," Henry shouted. "Once he's had you, he'll toss you aside like yesterday's garbage."

Alanna's hands were still shaking with fury when she walked into the inn. Despite her anger, she was aware of the stares and the gazes searing her. Yet, she felt no shame. She was going to the man she loved and that was all that mattered.

The inn's furniture was old and well worn, but the floors were swept clean and on the front desk there was a white enamel vase filled with fresh wildflowers. She walked up to the front desk where Sloan sat hunched over a ledger.

Sloan didn't look up from his register when he spoke. "That dandy ain't staying in my inn."

Alanna couldn't help but smile. "He's got his own coach. I'm sure he'll be gone within the hour."

Sloan peered over his glasses. "Way I hear it, that hired stage had a broken wheel. He's stuck here until morning."

"Henry won't like that." She bit her lip so she wouldn't smile.

"Good."

Sloan reached for a pen. He dipped the tip into a glass ink well. A drop of ink dropped from the nib before he started to scratch letters into the ledger.

Alanna looked around the lobby. There was no sign of Caleb. She felt awkward. A lady didn't ask an innkeeper the whereabouts of a single man. Nervous, she tapped her finger on the desk.

Sloan didn't look up. "You need something?"

He wasn't making this easy. "Mr. Sloan, where can I find Caleb?"

"Upstairs."

"May I ask what room?" She glanced up the stairs.

Sloan set down his pen. "Caleb's a good man."

Alanna stopped, her smile fading. "I know."

"Don't hurt him."

His candor shocked her. "I've no intention of hurting him."

"The road to hell is paved with good intentions." Before she could speak he held up his hand, silencing her. "He ain't told me a lot about what happened in Richmond, but I've pieced together enough. He might not ever say it but he loves you."

She stood her ground, her head held high. "We

both made mistakes in the past. We've learned from them.''

"Have you? This is a hard life here on the ocean. If you ain't up to it, walk away now.''

"I don't want to walk away.''

He snorted. "He'll get over you if you leave now. But if you start making promises and give that man hope, then you'll destroy him if you leave him again.''

Alanna loved Caleb. And she'd rather die than hurt him as she had before. She prayed for the strength to make Caleb a good wife. "I won't.''

He studied her a long moment. "Room one-twenty-one.''

"Thank you.''

She climbed the stairs. Lanterns hung from the dingy walls of the narrow, dark hallway carpeted with a fading red carpet. There were six doors on the right, five on the left and each was marked with faded black letters.

Excitement and trepidation surged through her limbs as she moved from door to door. The last door on the right was Caleb's.

Standing as still as a statue, she stared at the faded letters. Her heart hammered in her chest. She understood when she passed through this door, there'd be no turning back. She'd leave Richmond behind forever.

She wished she could say she wasn't afraid, but she was. Life with Caleb would be filled with adventure and passion, but it would not be an easy life. She prayed she had the courage to be what he needed.

Alanna reached for the door handle, turned it slowly and went into the room.

When she opened it, she found Caleb standing by the window staring across the calm sound waters toward the lighthouse. He'd taken off his dark blue jacket and now wore just a thick cotton shirt tucked into black pants cinched at the waist by a thick black belt. His boots were scuffed. His hands were clasped behind his back.

Tension gripped his broad shoulders. "Is he gone?"

As she stared at him, she realized she'd never loved him more. Her fears vanished.

He continued to stare out the window. "He can give you back everything you had and more."

She closed the door. "He can't give me what I really want."

"What do you want?" he said roughly.

She came up behind him and wrapped her arms around his chest. "You."

Caleb stiffened, turned and pulled away from her. "Alanna, think carefully about what you're giving up."

His sudden reserve puzzled her. "I have."

He stabbed long fingers through his thick hair. "I don't think you've thought it through."

"You've spent the last two days trying to convince me to stay. Why the hesitation now?"

"Henry. Looking at him made me realize how different your old life will be from your new one. Hell, his suit cost more than some men make here in a year. There'll be no more silks. No fancy parties. No private coaches. Life out here is hard."

She realized then she'd not been the only one who was afraid. "I don't want any more fancy parties. I've no desire ever to return to my old life again."

A cynical smile curved his lips. "You say that now, but time changes many things."

"It won't change my mind. I am certain."

He brushed a curl from her soft face. "The town looked so tired and worn compared to him."

"Easton possesses its own kind of beauty. It's approachable, real. I feel at home here. Good or bad, I know where I stand with the people here. I could never say the same about my old friends. And Henry's perfect appearance reminds me of a beautiful porcelain figurine. Cold and unapproachable."

"In time when the weather and hardships start

to wear on you, you could grow to resent this place.''

''I know it's not going to be easy.''

His voice mirrored the pain in his heart. ''You don't know how hard it can be.''

She kept her voice steady. She'd appeal to his logic. ''I know I've a history of acting impulsively. But this is no impulse. For the first time in a long time, it feels as if I've come home.''

His jaw tightened. ''My mother grew to hate this place.''

''I'm not like her.''

''She was an outsider like you. She was used to finer things. My father wanted her to be happy, but his duties took him away a lot. In the end, she resented the hell out of him. I don't want that to happen to us.'' He drew in a deep breath. ''I'd rather you leave now than see that happen.''

She moved over to the bed and sat down, staking her claim. ''I'm not leaving, Caleb.''

Caleb shook his head. ''If you stay the night, I won't be able to let you go.''

She crossed her legs, brazenly showing a bit of ankle. ''I'm counting on that.''

Caleb stared at her a long moment and then something inside of him seemed to snap. In two strides he closed the distance between them. He hauled her to her feet. "You are stubborn as a mule. Impulsive. Willful. You drive me insane."

She wrapped her arms loosely around his neck. "I know. Isn't it wonderful?"

He cupped Alanna's face with his large hands and kissed her fully on the lips. He tasted of salt and a hint of whiskey.

The tension melted from her body and she eased toward him, pressing her hands against his chest. A soft moan rumbled in her chest.

His hands dropped to her shoulders and he pulled her closer to him. He deepened the kiss.

His warmth ran the length of her body. Her insides turned to jelly. "Caleb."

He broke the kiss long enough to swoop her up in his arms. She fit in his arms as if she were meant to be here. Desire simmered inside her.

He carried her to the bed and laid her in the center. The fading afternoon light trickled through the window, deepening the lines at the corner of his eyes. The mattress sagged when he sat on the edge. He trailed his hand up and down her arm. He rubbed his hand over the smooth skin of her face. "You are the most beautiful woman."

She reached up and traced the scar on his face. "And you are the most handsome man."

He leaned forward and pushed her back into

the mattress. The weight of him felt good against her body. She felt alive.

"This is your last chance," he said. "A minute or two more and I won't let you go."

A seductive smile curved her lips. "Shut up and kiss me."

Chapter Seventeen

Caleb cupped Alanna's face in his hands. He stared into her eyes and savored the soft skin of her face. He'd dreamed about this moment so many times in the last two years. There'd been nights when he'd thought he'd go insane wanting her and here she was—with him now.

He kissed her on the lips, drinking in the taste of her. She wrapped her arms around his neck and pressed her breasts into his chest. A soft moan rumbled in the back of her throat.

His erection throbbed and he wanted nothing more than to drive into her. But he was determined to go slow. He wanted this moment to last. He wanted to enjoy every inch of her body.

He wove his fingers through her hair. It still felt like spun silk, but it did not have the perfumed scent of roses as it had two years ago. It smelled like a fresh breeze, sunshine.

Straddling her, Caleb trailed kisses down Alanna's face to her neck. He unhooked the top button on her bodice and kissed the soft skin at the hollow of her neck. She hissed in a breath and stared up at him with eyes full of wanting.

Nothing could make him want Alanna more.

He liked the play of passion on her face—desire, longing, heat—so he kept his gaze on her eyes as he unfastened the second and then the third button. She moistened her lips and wriggled under him. He thought he'd explode.

Caleb lowered his gaze and to his delight discovered she wore no chemise. "Alanna, no undergarments."

She blushed prettily. "It's indecent, I know. But there were none in the chest."

Chuckling, he kissed the bare skin above her breasts. "Ah, I like it better that you don't have anything on."

Her gaze darkened. "It is rather wicked of me, isn't it?"

"Aye, wicked."

Her throaty seductive laugh had his hands trembling as he unfastened three more buttons. Pushing back the soft fabric, he stared down at her naked breasts. He'd never seen a more erotic sight.

Banding her narrow waist with his hands, Caleb

lowered his face to a nipple and suckled until it grew hard.

Alanna arched. "You are driving me mad."

He smiled. "Good."

He trailed kisses down the center of her breasts and across her flat tummy to her navel.

She threaded her fingers through his hair. "Caleb, what are you doing to me?"

"Wait and see." He grabbed the hem of her skirt and pulled it up to her waist. No pantaloons! He had died and gone to heaven. He kissed lower.

Alanna knew the meaning of madness! The blood raced through her veins as if she were on fire. Caleb was kissing her in ways that didn't seem decent yet she couldn't bring herself to protest. She'd never felt more alive or wanted him more.

She didn't know how long he kept her teetering between madness and sanity, but when he rose up to pull off his shirt she heard herself whimper.

Pride had kept her going these last two years, but in the face of such longing, it vanished. She wanted him and was on the verge of begging for release.

He slid off his pants. Lantern light flickered on his muscled legs and flat belly. His body looked as if it were forged from marble—a Greek god in the form of a flesh-and-blood man.

Her gaze lowered to his arousal. She blushed.

Yes, they'd been together before, but when they'd made love it had always been completely dark. She'd felt him inside of her but she'd never *seen* him.

Caleb gave her no time to think or worry. He slid her dress off her shoulders. She lifted her backside as he pulled the garment over her hips. He tossed the dress on the floor next to his pants and sweater.

He lifted her leg and then kissed the curve of her calf still covered with a black stocking. He reached for her foot, and then unfastened the buttons on her ankle-high shoe. He jerked each button open with maddening slowness before he pulled off the shoe and tossed it on the floor.

She smoothed her hands down her flat belly and raised her other foot to him. Again, he unfastened each button slowly. One. Two. Three. Finally he pulled the shoe off and tossed it aside. His hands trailed up her calf and he slid the stocking off.

She was completely naked now. She felt wanton. Alive.

He covered her naked body with his. He stroked her hair. Kissed the hollow of her neck and then began to move lower to the soft peak of her breast. Rational thought vanished and instinct took over.

She opened her legs. His hard flesh pressed against her.

He groaned. "I want us to take our time."

Need collided with impulse. "You've taken enough time. I want you in me now."

The muscles in his neck tightened as if he wrestled to rein in his desire. "We've all night."

"Now," she urged.

What hold he had on his control seemed to snap. His eyes darkened with passion. He positioned himself at her entrance and then pushed into her, his gaze never leaving her face.

He moved slowly inside of her first until her tightness grew accustomed to him. The fires he'd stoked before flamed hotter.

And then in the next instant, she was engulfed in a wave of pleasure so strong and powerful that she lost all control. She arched and fisted handfuls of the sheets under her. She called out his name.

He drove into her, like a man possessed. His cries mingled with her own and for an instant their hearts beat as one.

He collapsed against her. She could feel his hot breath against her neck as his racing heart thrummed against her chest.

Finally, Caleb rolled on his back. Alanna wiggled her body close to his and laid her cheek on his chest. He wrapped his arm around her shoulder and held her close.

Never had life felt more right.

Never had she been so happy.

A clock chimed twice.

Caleb was gone.

These were the first rational thoughts Alanna had when she awoke. The room was awash in darkness except for the firelight flickering from the hearth.

The sheets felt cool against her skin when she sat up. She pushed the thick curtain of hair from her face and searched the room for Caleb. Had it been a dream? Had they really made love last night?

So many nights she'd had a dream just like last night. Only those mornings, when her mind cleared she realized she was alone.

"Caleb!" She detested the panic in her voice.

"Aye, I'm here." His deep voice came from a darkened corner. He stepped from the shadows near the window and moved toward the bed.

He wore only his pants. His black hair was tousled. He was smiling.

She sat up, unmindful that the sheet dropped away from her shoulders. Reaching out to him, she savored the touch of his bare skin. "I thought I'd been dreaming."

He took her hand in his and kissed her palm. "No dream."

She slid her hand up to his shoulder. "I've spent so long apart from you that I'm having trouble believing it's real."

He kissed her forehead. "It's real."

She closed her eyes and nuzzled her cheek against his. "I will never get tired of touching you."

"Good." His voice was deeper and possessed a seductive quality.

"What were you doing at the window? You must be exhausted."

He traced her nose with her fingertip. "Not so tired anymore."

Outside, the distant beacon of the lighthouse flashed. "Are you worried about the lighthouse?"

He shook his head. "No. My assistant is an able man. I've not slept the night through in so many years, I doubt I know how anymore."

His tone was light, but she sensed he was worried. The old connection they'd once shared had returned and felt stronger than before. "You are worried about something."

He kissed her. "What makes you say that?"

"The way your forehead creases. The way you purse your lips."

He laughed. "You think you know me so well?"

"Yes," she said. She refused to let him deflect the question. "Now tell me what is wrong."

He shook his head. "No worries."

Whatever doubts plagued him, he wasn't ready to talk about them. She'd endured a lifetime of fears in the last two years and she wanted to talk about them and banish all traces of them, but she knew he wasn't ready.

She would respect his privacy.

But that didn't mean she didn't want to make love to him. What she couldn't say to him in words, she could express with her body.

Normally she could be very direct and speak her mind. But in these matters of the bedroom, she still felt a bit shy.

Alanna had promised herself she'd not act so impulsively anymore. But this time she felt that if she didn't plunge in, she'd lose her nerve.

Without a second thought, she took his hand and guided him to the bed. "It's my turn this time."

"What do you have in mind?" His voice was as rough as sand and barnacles.

She rolled on top of him and straddled his narrow hips. Her long hair trailed over her breast like a curtain. Trailing a finger down his naked belly, she reached for his belt buckle.

He pushed her hair behind her shoulder, his gaze locked on her. He brushed the underside of her breast with his knuckle. Her nipple hardened before she brushed his hand away. "Sit back and relax."

Cupping her naked buttocks with his hand, he laughed. "Lady, I couldn't relax now if you paid me."

She unhooked his belt buckle and unfastened the first button. "Good."

Caleb sucked in a breath when she slid her fingers below his pants line. "Alanna," he groaned.

Savoring her womanly power over him, she unfastened three more buttons. "The first time we were together, I wanted to do this. But everything was so new to me I didn't dare try." She took hold of him. Kissed him. Enjoyed the sharp hiss of breath through his clenched teeth. "I will never lack courage again."

Caleb didn't speak. He threaded his fingers through her hair and endured the sweet torture. Finally, he reached breaking point. He took hold of her shoulders, pulled her up and then turned her over on her back.

She opened her legs to him and he drove into

her with the force of a man possessed. Sensations swept them both up and washed over them. In the end, they collapsed against each other—their bodies soaked in sweat and satiated.

Just before dawn, Caleb awoke again. He rolled on his side, propped his head up on his hand and stared down at her.

If it were possible, time had made her more beautiful.

He studied the bridge of her nose. The sun yesterday had deepened her freckles and tinged her white skin with a bit of pink. Soon the color would darken to a rich brown. The color would fade in the winter. A lightkeeper's wife rarely had time for parasols. Bonnets offered some protection but in time the sun took its toll on delicate skin. In five or ten years, the sun's rays would etch tiny lines by her eyes and mouth.

He pictured her in his mind's eye and knew that no matter what, he would love her. She was his heart; his soul.

But would she be happy with the changes such a hard life brought?

Alanna's eyes fluttered open. She smiled up at him. "What are you thinking about?"

He captured a silken curl in his hands. "The future."

She smiled. "The future. That sounds so nice, doesn't it? For so long I didn't think past putting one foot in front of the other. The end of each day was as far as I could see."

"Aye." He understood exactly what she was saying.

A cloud of sadness had her frowning before she visibly shook it off. "But I'm not thinking about *those* days anymore. We are talking about tomorrow and the day after that and the day after that." She ran her hand along his leg. "You know what I see in our future? Lots of children."

Alanna mothering his children—the idea appealed to him. "How many?"

"Five or six. And I see boys just like you running up and down the beach with Toby."

Caleb chuckled. "Toby does like children. I've seen the children in the village hang on him and smother him with hugs and he patiently takes it all."

"And maybe there will be a daughter or two."

He cocked an eyebrow. "Eight children. That's a tall order."

Her hand slid below the sheet. "I've no doubt you can handle it."

He rolled on top of her. "You know at the rate we are going, you're going to kill me." Already he was hard and pressing against her entrance.

She lifted her hips to him. "Can you think of a better way to go?"

He slid into her. "Not a one."

An hour later, the room was awash in bright sunshine. Alanna could hear the patrons of the inn stirring. The outside world was waiting for them and like it or not, this fantasy night with Caleb was coming to an end.

She rose up and swung her legs over the side of the bed. Her foot landed on her dress, still heaped on top of Caleb's shirt. Lifting the dress, she shook out the wrinkles.

Caleb stirred. "What are you doing?"

"This dress is a mess and in desperate need of pressing."

He hooked his arm around her waist and pulled her back. "You don't need clothes."

Laughing she wrestled free. "I will if I hope to catch the coach."

"Coach." Tension radiated from his voice.

She realized then that he, too, wasn't immune to the fear. "I need to see the Randalls before they go. I owe them both the truth."

Relaxing, he nodded.

"Don't worry, nothing can lure me back to Richmond permanently. This is my home now, but there is a practical side to all this. I have clothes and some furniture that I must fetch.''

He took her in his arms and held on to her as if he were afraid she'd slip away. ''There's no need for you to return to Richmond at all. We'll send for your possessions or I'll buy you what you need.''

On cue her stomach rumbled. Pressing her hand to her belly she laughed. ''You're going to have to feed me sooner or later.''

He laughed and sat up. ''Aye, I could use a bit of food myself.''

Alanna started to rise. ''I'll go and fetch us something to eat.''

''Don't move,'' Caleb ordered, pressing her back against the pillows. ''I'll go downstairs and have Sloan fix us a hearty breakfast.''

''I'll come with you.''

''Stay. I like the idea of coming back to my room and finding you in bed.''

Smiling, she watched him dress. He saluted her before he left and promised to return soon.

Lord, but she loved that man.

Her love burned just as hot as it had two years ago, but this time it was different. Two years ago, her love had been untested and fragile, born more out of a fantasy than reality.

The love she felt for him today was stronger. It had endured a trial by fire and risen from the ashes more powerful than before.

Nothing would ever tear them apart again.

Chapter Eighteen

For the first time in years Caleb looked forward to tomorrow with hope. A half smile curved his lips as he strode downstairs into the inn. The place was quiet. Sloan was nowhere to be found.

He moved to the bar and drummed his fingers against the polished wood. Alanna was in his bed waiting for him. And he was in a rush to return to her.

"I'm almost glad she's staying."

Henry's voice had the muscles in Caleb's back tensing. Turning, he found the man pushing through the front door. Dark circles hung under Henry's pale green eyes. His suit, normally meticulously pressed, was wrinkled.

Caleb's impatience doubled as he watched Henry stride into the room. Henry represented the past and he wanted nothing more to do with the past. "I'll take that as your blessing."

Henry tugged his coat jacket over a soiled cuff. "You were always a pain in my side. From the moment you stepped onto the docks at Patterson."

Caleb's jaw tensed. "Why haven't you left Easton yet?"

His eyes narrowed. "My coach I hired, which was in perfect working condition yesterday, now has a broken wheel. The only man in town who could fix it was away yesterday. I was forced to spend the night sitting up in a godforsaken tavern waiting for him."

Sloan at work, Caleb mused. He'd bet next month's salary that Sloan had told him there were no rooms in his inn. He'd also bet Henry would pay five times the rate for the return trip. "Bad luck."

Henry sneered. "Bad luck has nothing to do with it. Your locals have been at work. Seems they think a lot of you."

"Make your point."

Henry strode behind the bar as if he owned it and grabbed a glass and a bottle of whisky. He filled the glass full. "I can think of no better place that Alanna deserves than Easton."

Silent, Caleb stood rigid. "You better go."

Henry drained his glass. He winced and coughed. "In five years, she'll be just as tired and broken as this run-down town.'' Henry tapped a smooth finger on the edge of his glass. ''She's so impulsive. We both know that. She'll spend the rest of her days wishing she'd stayed with me.''

Caleb wasn't ashamed of himself or the life he'd chosen. But standing this close to Henry he was keenly aware of his rough hands callused by hard work. His coat was well worn and his boots scuffed. This life suited him fine, but again he worried if it was for Alanna?

''You know I'm right,'' Henry said. Like an animal that sensed doubt, he moved in to kill. ''You are a pariah in polite society. You lost your ship. Good men died because you could not do your job. Once Alanna marries you, she'll have to bear your shame.''

Fury scorched Caleb's soul. He moved so close to Henry that their boot tips touched. ''Get on that stage and leave this town now.'' There was a dangerous edge to his voice.

Henry heard it. Paling, he took a step back. Then turning abruptly he hurried to the door and opened it. ''In the end she will hate you.'' He slammed the door behind him.

In the quiet stillness, Caleb let the tension seep from his shoulders. The exhilaration he'd felt moments ago had vanished. The bitterness returned.

Sloan walked through the kitchen door, drying

his hands with a towel. "Don't tell me I heard that Henry Strathmore's voice. You'd have thought that whelp would stay clear of me." He chuckled. "Nate did a number on the man's carriage wheel."

Sloan pulled a tray out from under the bar. "Got some hotcakes on the grill. Be happy to send a tray up."

Caleb traced the edge of the tray with his thumb. "This is a hard life we live out here."

Sloan rubbed the back of his neck with his hand. "Aye," he said.

"It's hardest on the women."

Sensing the direction of his thoughts, Sloan's eyes narrowed. "She's tougher than I ever gave her credit for. When she first came to town, I'd have bet the bar she'd not travel across the waters to see you. But she did."

"She nearly got herself killed doing it."

"Life ain't easy out here, Caleb."

"Do you think she will grow to hate this place?"

"She sure did love it yesterday."

He heard the hesitation in the old man's voice. "Yes or no, Sloan. Do you think she has what it takes?"

Sloan shook his head. "I think she loves you."

Caleb knew she'd stay with him no matter

what. But was she better off living somewhere
where the wind, sun and salt air didn't eat away
at you. "That's not what I asked."

Sloan muttered an oath. "I don't know. Only
time will tell."

Caleb knew Alanna would give this place her
best try. She'd work hard. She wouldn't complain.
But when he looked deep into his heart, he found
himself face-to-face with old doubts. His mother
had grown to despise this place. It had drained the
life from her. He didn't want to see that happen
to Alanna.

It was only ten o'clock—too early for liquor,
but he had a powerful taste for whiskey.

Sloan must have sensed what he was thinking.
He set two fresh glasses on the bar and filled
them. "You love her?"

Caleb drowned his in one swallow. "Aye."

"Then I say make the best of it. Hell, who
knows, she could do just fine out here."

Caleb pictured Alanna when he'd last seen her
in Richmond. She'd been dressed in silks and
she'd breezed through the ballroom as if she
didn't have a care in the world. He tried to picture
her in ten years. Images of Alanna's smiling face
collided with his last memory of his mother's
tired features. His father had refused to let his

mother go and the results had been hell for everyone.

He set the glass down. "I can't do it to her."

"Do what?"

"Ask her to stay."

Alanna waited in the room for Caleb for nearly an hour. Finally, she began to worry, so she dressed quickly. She combed her fingers through her long hair and braided it. Moving to the door, she glanced back at the bed, still rumpled from their night of lovemaking.

Abruptly, she was struck by a feeling of dread. Caleb wouldn't leave her like this. Something was terribly wrong.

When she arrived downstairs, the inn was full of customers. Sloan was busy behind the bar, loading plates of flapjacks onto a tray.

She went directly to him. "Where is he?"

Sloan hoisted the tray up on his arm. "Henry left."

"I'm not talking about Henry! I'm talking about Caleb."

"He's gone." Sloan moved around the bar and wove between the tables. He served three fishermen and started back toward the bar.

Alanna blocked his path. *"Where is he?"*

Sloan dropped his gaze. "Gone back to the lighthouse."

"Without me? When will he be back?"

"I don't reckon he is coming back."

Stunned, she stood there. It was just as Henry had said. He'd left her.

When Caleb strode into the lightkeeper's cottage, he was struck by the solitude. He heard the clock tick on the parlor mantle, the wind whistle past the house, and the waves crashing in the distance.

Toby rose from his bed by the stove and sauntered over to Caleb. The dog sniffed his fingers then moved past Caleb as if he were searching for Alanna.

He'd never felt so alone.

He shrugged off his coat and strode toward his office. There was bottle of whiskey in the bottom drawer. He shoved open the door and slammed it behind him. The windows rattled.

He sat down and yanked open the drawer and pulled out the bottle. He tossed the cork aside and took a long drink.

The brew tasted bitter and only managed to foul his bad mood.

A faint scratching echoed at the office door. "Go away, Toby!"

The dog scratched harder.

Irritated, he rose and opened the door. The dog sauntered past him as if he owned the place and sat down next to Caleb's desk.

"I'm foul company today. You're better to stay clear of me for a long time."

The dog barked.

"She's not coming back if that's what you're asking. The stage is leaving about now. She had no choice but to be on it."

From the corner of his eye, he saw the box Alanna had carried here for him. Snarling, he picked it up. Thanks to Obadiah Patterson, his world had been turned upside down. His fingers tightened around the box and he hurled it across the room. It smashed into the door and fell to the ground, shattered.

Alanna planted her hands on her hips. "I swear, Sloan, I will start screaming like a madwoman if you don't take me across the sound."

The buzz of conversation in the dining room went silent.

Sloan's expression looked pained. "He thinks it's best you two go your separate ways. He thinks you'll be happier in Richmond." His arms loaded with another tray of food, he tried to move around her.

She blocked him. "He's wrong!"

Sloan shoved out a sigh. "Is he? Take a good look around this room and at the people. If you stay you'll be as hard as they are in fifteen years."

"I don't care!"

"You say that now. I remember how rough it was for Caleb's parents. His ma loved this place when they arrived that first spring. By the time she died, she couldn't even look at the water because she hated the sight of it so much. Caleb's mother made life hell for everyone who came in close contact with her."

Alanna felt as though she was talking to a rock. "Hell? She made life hell!" She grabbed a plate of scrambled eggs and grits. She smashed it against the floor. "You and everyone else in this town don't know the meaning of the word *hell* until you've met an unhappy Alanna Patterson."

Sloan stared at the plate. A couple of the sailors and fishermen started to laugh. "What the devil has gotten into you?"

She grabbed another plate and held it high over her head. "Are you going to take me to the island?"

Sloan's gaze narrowed. "No."

Alanna slammed the plate onto the floor, covering Sloan's boots with pancakes. "Take me to Caleb."

"You're a madwoman."

"You've yet to see me really mad, Mr. Sloan. I can assure you it's a sight you don't want to see."

Sloan turned back to the bar and set the tray with the remaining plates out of her reach. "I promised him I wouldn't take you."

"This is so stupid. I want to be with him. I love him." Tears of frustration ran down her face as she turned to the crowd of men and women. "Won't anyone take me?"

The room grew silent and she was aware that all eyes had shifted to her. "I need to go to the lighthouse. Won't anyone help me?"

"Give it up," Sloan said. "It's best to let go now."

Soft murmurs rippled through the room.

"I don't have any money," Alanna said. "But I must get to the island to see Caleb. *Please.*"

A long silence passed before a fisherman with skin as rough as leather and a graying beard stood. He tossed his napkin on his half-eaten food. "I'll take you."

Sloan wagged his finger at the man. "Danny Walters. Don't you dare take her anywhere except back to Richmond. Caleb don't want her."

Alanna's heart raced. "He does want me! He's just worried."

Danny picked up his duffel bag. "Ida told me she had a vision about this gal. Said she and the captain was going to have four children. Three boys and a girl."

Sloan groaned. "Ida don't know what she's saying."

Another fisherman rose. Younger, he had a slim build and a deeply tanned face. "Ida says she's good for the captain then that's good enough for me." He touched his stocking cap. "Name's Bart Moore. If Danny won't take you I will."

Alanna clasped his hand. "Thank you."

Bart winked at her. "A woman's got to be a little crazy to take him on."

Another sailor rose. "Aye, I'd say she's just what the captain ordered."

Sloan groaned. "I don't want to see you two get hurt."

Alanna took his hand. "It will be all right."

He shook his head. "I hope you aren't making a mistake."

"I'm not."

Caleb stared at what was left of the box. It had broken into three pieces—two small, the other large. He'd have left the pieces of wood there if he'd not spotted the edge of paper sticking out from the large piece.

"What the hell?"

He rose and moved toward the box. Squatting, he picked up the yellowed paper rolled into a thin scroll banded with a thin cord.

He untied the band and unrolled the paper. The gold bracelet he'd once given Alanna fell to the floor. He picked it up. It glistened in the sunlight.

Caleb dropped his gaze to the letter. The handwriting was shaky and uneven, but there was no mistaking that it was a note from Obadiah to him.

Caleb, forgive an old man's greed. I never meant for anyone to die. My sins are unpardonable, but you must forgive yourself.

I've made so many mistakes that can't be righted but I can try to fix the damage I did to you and Alanna. There is no life in her when you two are apart. I know that now. You belong together. Take care of her. O.P.

Caleb reread the note several times. His brain turned the words over and over. And then a fierce tidal wave of emotions swept over him.

He tipped his head back, damning the tears that pooled in his eyes. He'd been so sure the old man had sent Alanna to destroy him. Instead, he'd been sending her to love him.

You belong together.

Once he'd damned Alanna for not having the courage to stand by his side, yet he was the one that now lacked courage. He'd sent her away because he'd been afraid.

He took several deep breaths until he felt a measure of control return. The fear drained from his body and his mind cleared.

Aye, he and Alanna belonged together.

"And I've let her go!" he shouted.

He rose and snatched up his coat, shoving the bracelet in his pocket. Toby lumbered to his feet. Wagging his tail he started to bark.

"You're right, I've been a damn fool." Mentally he calculated the stage route. They'd be an hour outside of town now. It would take him an hour to row to shore and another half hour to find a horse. If he were lucky, he'd catch up to her by nightfall before she got onto the barge to Richmond.

Damn, why did he let her go?

Like the devil himself was on his heels he ran down the hallway and out the back door as he shrugged on his coat. He raced down the pathway that led to the small sound-side dock where he'd tied his dory.

The sun was bright and the sun warm. He climbed down the dock ladder into the boat and reached for the knot. He yanked it loose and cast away from the dock.

His back to the mainland, he started to row. "Hang on, Alanna, I'm coming back to you."

The boat cut through the waters as he pumped the oars. He felt more and more anxious as each second ticked by. He couldn't make the boat move any faster and the frustration drove him to work harder.

Any other day he'd have savored the sight of the clear blue sky. He'd have paused to listen to the cry of the gulls and inhale the savory salt air.

It was a perfect day.

It was an awful day.

Sweat started to trickle down his back. He needed to stop rowing for a moment and shrug off his coat but didn't dare waste the time.

"Caleb."

He imagined Alanna's voice trailing on the winds. But of course, it couldn't be her. She was halfway to Coinjock Bay. Dear Lord, he wanted it to be her.

"Caleb!"

This time he stopped rowing and turned. Bright sunshine blinded him, forcing him to squint. He cupped his hand over his eyes.

He saw Alanna sitting in the bow of Sloan's

dory, her arms waving. Sunlight glistened on her blond hair. Her skirt billowed in the breeze.

It was as if the gods of the ocean granted his one and only wish. "Alanna!"

She beamed. "Caleb Pitt, if you think you are going to get rid of me that easily, you are sadly mistaken, sir."

God, he loved her. He rowed harder until his boat grazed the side of Sloan's. On one side of Sloan sat Danny and on the other Bart. All three looked winded, ready to collapse, as if Alanna had driven them hard.

His gaze shifted to Alanna. Her eyes were red with tears.

He held out his hands to her and immediately she leaned toward him. He hugged his arms around her and lifted her into his boat. "I was a fool."

She hugged him tight, and then she kissed his face. "Don't ever do that to me again."

He kissed her on the lips. "You're stuck with me, Alanna. Nothing's going to tear us apart again."

Sloan wiped the sweat from his forehead. "You'd do me a great service, Captain, if you'd marry the woman. She broke half the dishes in my inn. I'll tell you now, I'm far too old for such dramatics."

Danny jabbed Bart in the ribs. "Don't you believe it, Caleb. I ain't seen that old man move so fast in years. Got his blood pumping."

"Thank you all," Caleb said.

They nodded, proud of themselves. "We'd do anything for you, Captain."

Caleb gazed into Alanna's warm eyes. "I'll marry the lady if she'll have me."

Her eyes glistened, reflecting all the love in her heart. "I'll marry him. It's forever and always, Captain Pitt."

"Aye, forever and always."

Epilogue

June, 1894

Nine-year-old Nathan Pitt squirmed as his mother wiped the last traces of milk from the corner of his mouth. "Mom, ssstopp! I look fine."

Alanna couldn't help but smile as she stared down at her firstborn child who of all her three boys looked so much like Caleb. "Your father went to a lot of trouble to arrange for the photographer and bring him out to the island, so I want this family portrait to be perfect."

"I look fine," he groaned.

She swiped the last bit of milk off his upper lip. "Now you do." She glanced over to the row of chairs lined up in front of the lightkeeper's cottage, which had been her home these last ten years.

Pride swelled in her as she stared at the cottage's whitewashed wood. Yellow morning glories in full bloom draped over the side of white window boxes. Two rockers now sat on the front porch and behind the house was a vegetable garden. Two cows grazed near a chicken pen filled with chickens that pecked at the dirt.

They'd become self-sufficient, she and Caleb and their brood.

"Dad's waving to us," Nathan said.

Alanna turned and saw Caleb striding toward them. He wore his keeper's blue uniform, its brass buttons shining in the sunlight. In his arms he held their daughter, eight-month-old Casey. Their six-year-old Kevin and four-year-old Aaron trotted beside him.

She smiled. Each time she looked at him her breath caught in her throat. He still had the power to make her knees weak.

"Alanna, the photographer is ready." Caleb caught Kevin's hand as he reached for a handful of sand. "We better hurry. I don't know how much longer this crew is going to stay clean."

She laughed, accepting Casey as the babe leaned toward her. The child grinned, revealing her four new teeth. "Then let us get going, Mr. Pitt."

The boys ran ahead toward the row of chairs the photographer had lined in front of the cottage.

Alanna and Caleb hung back. He wrapped his arm around her waist and hugged her close. ''I'm not sure if I said it yet today, but I love you, Mrs. Pitt.''

She savored his warmth, his love, his touch. Already she thought ahead to tonight when the children would be put to bed and they'd be alone. ''And I love you, Mr. Pitt.''

* * * * *

HEAD FOR THE ROCKIES WITH

Harlequin Historicals®
Historical Romantic Adventure!

AND SEE HOW IT ALL BEGAN!

COLORADO CONFIDENTIAL

**Check out these three historicals
connected to the bestselling Intrigue series**

CHEYENNE WIFE
by Judith Stacy
January 2004

COLORADO COURTSHIP
by Carolyn Davidson
February 2004

ROCKY MOUNTAIN MARRIAGE
by Debra Lee Brown
March 2004

Available at your favorite retail outlet.

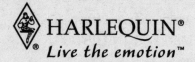

HARLEQUIN®
Live the emotion™

Visit us at www.eHarlequin.com

TAKE A TRIP TO THE OLD WEST WITH FOUR HANDSOME HEROES FROM HARLEQUIN HISTORICALS

On sale March 2004

ROCKY MOUNTAIN MARRIAGE
by Debra Lee Brown

Chance Wellesley
Rogue and gambler

MAGGIE AND THE LAW
by Judith Stacy

Spence Harding
Town sheriff

On sale April 2004

THE MARRIAGE AGREEMENT
by Carolyn Davidson

Gage Morgan
Undercover government agent

BELOVED ENEMY
by Mary Schaller

Major Robert Montgomery
U.S. Army major, spy

Visit us at www.eHarlequin.com

HARLEQUIN HISTORICALS®

HHWEST30

COMING NEXT MONTH FROM
HARLEQUIN HISTORICALS®

- **ROCKY MOUNTAIN MARRIAGE**
  by **Debra Lee Brown,** the third of three historicals in the
  Colorado Confidential series
  After discovering she'd inherited a saloon from her estranged father,
  a straitlaced schoolteacher travels to Colorado. When a mysterious
  gambler takes a shine to her, will she open her heart to love?
  HH #695 ISBN# 29295-3 $5.25 U.S./$6.25 CAN.

- **THE NORMAN'S BRIDE**
  by **Terri Brisbin,** author of THE DUMONT BRIDE
  Thought dead and killed in battle, Sir William De Severin is in truth
  alive and lives as a mercenary. When he finds a noblewoman left for
  dead in the forest, he nurses her back to health…but will this mean
  confronting the life he had long abandoned?
  HH #696 ISBN# 29296-1 $5.25 U.S./$6.25 CAN.

- **RAKE'S REWARD**
  by **Joanna Maitland,** the sequel to MARRYING THE MAJOR
  After five years of enforced exile, the black sheep of the Stratton
  family has returned to England, determined to have his revenge on
  the countess who ruined him at cards. But the countess has acquired
  a surprisingly beautiful companion who isn't fooled by his charming
  facade….
  HH #697 ISBN# 29297-X $5.25 U.S./$6.25 CAN.

- **MAGGIE AND THE LAW**
  by **Judith Stacy,** author of CHEYENNE WIFE
  Desperate to recover a priceless artifact, a young woman travels out
  west, only to learn that if she wants it back, she'll have to steal it! But
  how can she when the town's oh-so-handsome sheriff won't let her out
  of his sight?
  HH #698 ISBN# 29298-8 $5.25 U.S./$6.25 CAN.

KEEP AN EYE OUT FOR ALL FOUR
OF THESE TERRIFIC NEW TITLES

HHCNM0204